Iva Honeysuckle

MEETS
her
MATCH

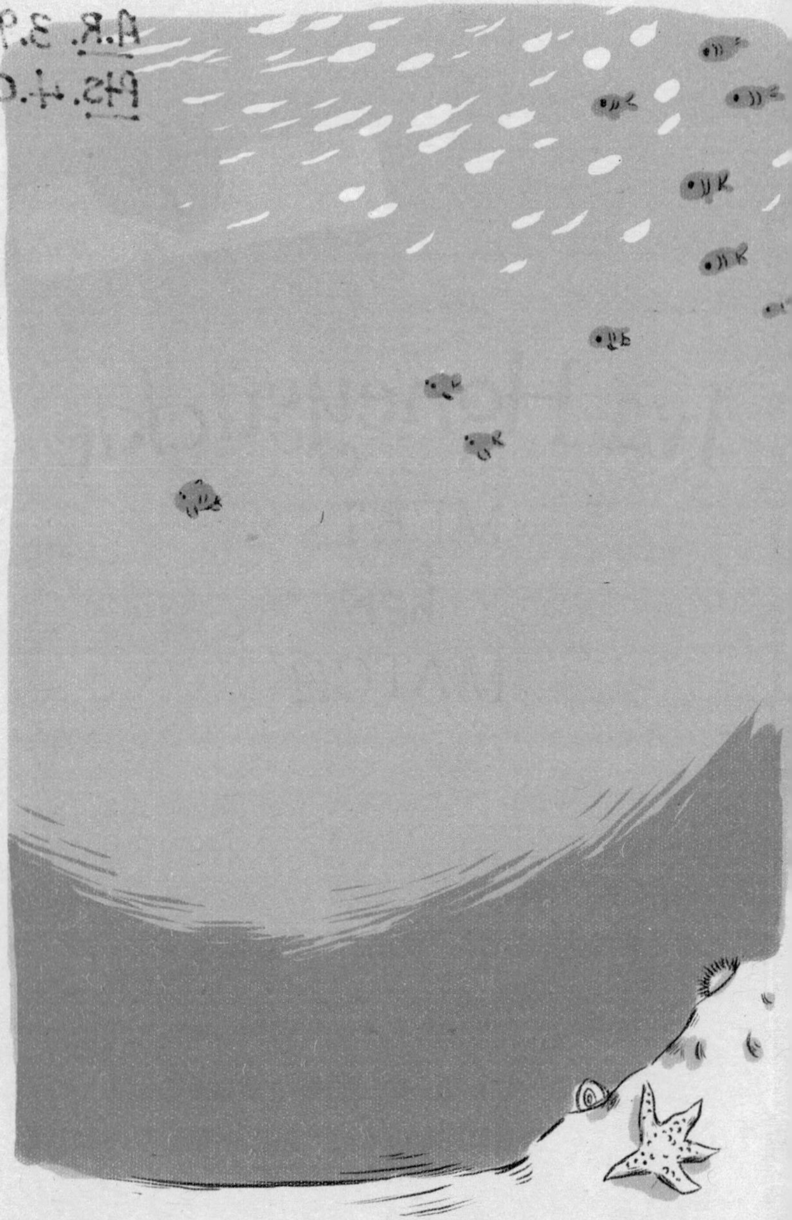

Iva Honeysuckle

MEETS
her
MATCH

By Candice Ransom

Illustrated by Heather Ross

Disney · HYPERION

Los Angeles | New York

Text copyright © 2013 by Candice Ransom

Illustrations copyright © 2013 by Heather Ross

First Hyperion paperback edition, 2014.
1 3 5 7 9 10 8 6 4 2
V475-2873-0 14231
Printed in the United States of America

Library of Congress Control Number for Hardcover Edition: 2012035111

ISBN 978-1-4231-3516-6

Visit www.DisneyBooks.com

SUSTAINABLE
FORESTRY
INITIATIVE

Certified Chain of Custody
Promoting Sustainable Forestry

www.sfiprogram.org
SFI-01054

The SFI label applies to the text stock

For Donna
friend-cousin-sister
with love

Chapter One

The All-Girl-Plus-One-Boy Trip of a Lifetime

Iva Honeycutt watched her cousin Heaven pull a card from her Daily Life deck. Heaven looked at the pink index card and frowned.

"What's it say?" Iva asked, interested in spite of herself.

"Make a soap dish from the lid of an oatmeal box." Heaven shoved the card back into the deck. "I don't feel like doing that today."

"Who would?" Iva said. "I thought you wrote those cards yourself. Why would you put in something so dumb?"

Heaven shuffled the index cards. Iva noticed she was quite skilled at it. She wondered if her cousin might secretly be part of the thirteen-year-old poker game held every Friday night in the basement of the Odd Fellows Lodge. Iva's father played in that game when he wasn't driving his big rig all over the country.

"Some days I wouldn't mind making a soap dish out of an oatmeal-box lid," Heaven explained. "But not today." She drew another card.

"Hey, that's cheating!"

"No, it's not. I made up the rules. And the rules say I can pick another card." Heaven smiled as she read her own neat printing. *Pack for a long trip.*

Iva fell over laughing on Heaven's bed. "A long trip! That's a good one!"

Heaven lived right next door, in a house not fifteen feet from Iva's. Iva could look out her bedroom window and watch her cousin water her African violets. Heaven was the only nine-year-old Iva knew who kept houseplants.

Iva had a plant in her room too—a fake tree that never needed watering. She pinned scraps of paper with names to the leaves. The names of people who were nice to Iva were pinned on leaves at the top of the tree. People Iva disliked stayed at the bottom.

Recently, Heaven's name had been promoted from the bottom to a spot near the middle of the tree, which meant Iva was getting along with her at the moment. One little slip, though, and Heaven would be demoted again.

"You are not going on any long trip!" Iva said. "We never go anywhere. We will be stuck in this town for the rest of our lives."

This was a sore spot with Iva. She was a discoverer, and discoverers went places. Iva had never been outside of Uncertain, Virginia, except to go to Dawn and Central Garage, the next two towns over. And Central Garage wasn't even a town—it was just a garage.

"How do you know I'm not taking a long trip?" Heaven sniffed loudly. She had adenoids and bad sinuses. "I'm almost ten. I could go on trips."

"I'm almost ten too," Iva said. "In"—she counted in her head—"eleven and a half months."

"Oh, please," Heaven said in a pitying tone. "I didn't tell you everything on that card. Like where I'm going. Sit up. You're wrinkling my best chenille bedspread."

Iva decided to shift Heaven's name back down to the bottom of her tree. It wasn't Iva's fault she was younger than her double-first cousin. Iva's mother and Heaven's mother were sisters who had married the Honeycutt brothers. If their mothers had had their way, Iva and Heaven would have been born on the very same day.

"So, where are you going on this big trip?" She spit on her index finger to twist the tufts on Heaven's bedspread into little peaks.

"Luray Caverns," Heaven said, as if the world were her oyster.

Iva knew that the famous Luray Caverns had been discovered a long time ago by a teenage boy and his uncle. She dreamed of making an important discovery like that.

Iva's father had visited Luray Caverns when he was Iva's age. He had told her about the organ made out of stalactites that played real songs. And Skeleton's Gorge, scattered with the bones of ancient people, and Giant's Hall, and Elfin Ramble.

And now Heaven was going. At least her Daily Life card predicted she would be. Iva was acid with envy.

Heaven opened her dresser drawer and began taking out shorts and T-shirts. She stacked them on the bed beside Iva.

"I'll need a sweatshirt," she said, sounding like she was fifty. "I hear it's always chilly in the caverns."

"You don't even know where the caverns are."

"Do so!"

"Do not!" Then Iva added, "I can find it on my globe."

For getting all Bs on her report card, Iva had received a small tin globe that was also a bank. It had belonged to her father when he was a little boy. His grandfather, Ludwell Honeycutt, had given it to him.

The Pacific Ocean was dented and somebody had spilled shoe polish on the North Pole. Iva loved the globe because it came from her great-grandfather, a discoverer like her, and because of the strange countries like French Indochina and the Belgian Congo. She couldn't find those countries in the atlas at the library.

"I'll find the caverns for you," Iva said, "for a fee."

"A fee!" Heaven snorted. She was a mouth-breather and could snort like a registered hog. "Like I'd pay money to see your tacky old globe that I can look at any time I want."

Iva kept the globe on her dresser, along with Ludwell Honeycutt's geography-bee medal and other treasures. The top of Heaven's dresser was littered with bottles of cheap perfume with names like Morning Glory and Pretty Peach.

"My globe is a lot better than your crummy bottles of toilet water," Iva said. "You spray that stuff on and stink to high Heaven. Hee-hee!" She laughed at her own joke.

Heaven huffed with her left nostril. "If anybody stinks, it's you. I'll have you know I've almost got enough perfume to wear a different smell every hour of the day."

Iva was bored. "Let's get something to eat." She rocketed from Heaven's bedroom into the kitchen.

Iva's mother was sitting at the table with Heaven's mother, drinking iced tea. They murmured over numbers scratched on the back of Howard's Big Chief tablet. A plate of Toll House cookies lay between them.

Heaven snatched a cookie and asked her mother, "What're you-all doing?"

"Figuring," Aunt Sissy Two replied. "Sissy," she said to Iva's mother. "If we rent this house, Howard can sleep on the sofa bed and—"

Just then, Iva's little sister, Lily Pearl, trudged in backward, dragging Howard by one arm across the floor. Lily Pearl wore an old lace curtain pinned on the top of her head. Howard was as limp as a dishrag, and his eyes were closed.

Aunt Sissy Two jumped up. "Howard, honey! What happened?"

"Nothing," said Lily Pearl. "Howard won't marry me, so we wrestled. I won."

Iva wasn't surprised. Spindly Lily Pearl appeared to be whipped up from toothpicks, but she was strong for a five-year-old.

Lily Pearl dropped Howard's arm. "Aunt Sissy Two, do you have any rice? You're supposed to throw rice when people get married."

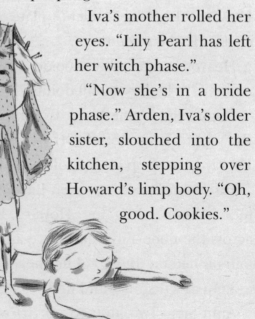

Iva's mother rolled her eyes. "Lily Pearl has left her witch phase."

"Now she's in a bride phase." Arden, Iva's older sister, slouched into the kitchen, stepping over Howard's limp body. "Oh, good. Cookies."

Hunter came in behind Arden. Always as famished as wolves, the girls grabbed fistfuls of cookies.

"Rory loves Toll House cookies," Arden said to Hunter. "They're his favorite."

"We should bake some and send him a box!" said Hunter.

"How can he eat them?" Iva asked. "He doesn't exist."

Arden flashed Iva a withering glance. "You're far too childish to understand affairs of the heart."

"If this Rory guy was real, which he isn't, he wouldn't be caught dead with a couple of twelve-year-olds," Iva said. But she was glad Arden had quit her summer project of screeching Johnny Cash songs on her alto sax.

Hunter's summer project—reading all the Nancy Drew mysteries in order—was at least quieter than Arden's. Then they dreamed up this imaginary boyfriend named Rory, who couldn't decide which one he was going to ask out on a date. Every day, he changed his imaginary mind.

Sitting back down, Aunt Sissy Two poked Iva's mother. "Sometimes I think we should have thought twice before we had our babies together."

"We should have thought twice before we had babies, period," said Iva's mother.

If Iva had been around back then, she would have told them their Grand Plan wouldn't work. How could they have three sets of almost-the-exact-same-age double-first girl cousins who would be best friends with each other? For one thing, one of the planned-on girls turned out to be a boy, Howard.

Yet Arden and Hunter were best, best friends. They did everything together. Lily Pearl and Howard were tighter than ticks on a yard dog's back. Iva liked Heaven sometimes. She wasn't quite ready to claim Heaven as her best, best friend. She and Heaven had nothing in common.

Aunt Sissy Two sketched a flower on the tablet. "Maybe it's a mistake to put Heaven and Iva on the sleeping porch. You know how they are."

"What sleeping porch?" asked Heaven.

Iva's mother said, "I think they'll be all right. They're getting along better."

"What's a sleeping porch?" asked Lily Pearl. "Does it ever wake up?"

"Why do I have to sleep on a porch with Heaven?" Iva slid her question in sideways. That's the way it was at Heaven's house. Everybody talking at once. It was like that at her house, too.

Her mother ignored her. "You know, Sissy, if we want a real good time, we should leave the kids home."

"Shoot." Aunt Sissy Two flipped the pencil across the table. "Let's send the kids, and we'll stay home!" They cackled like a couple of setting hens.

"What," Arden demanded, "are you talking about?"

"It's been so hot this summer," Iva's mother answered. "We're going away for five days. Just us girls—"

Howard's eyes flew open. "Hey!"

"—plus one boy," Aunt Sissy Two finished. "Since Buddy and Uncle Sonny can't take off work, we decided we could manage a few days somewhere with you kids."

"But we're rethinking the whole thing," Iva's mother said, teasing.

"Aunt Sissy!" Hunter said.

"Don't worry. We're going. All of us." Iva's mother gently bopped Howard on the head with the tablet. "Even you, Peanut."

Iva nearly fainted. She was finally getting out of Uncertain! She needed to know immediately where they were going.

Heaven beat her to it. "We're going to the Luray Caverns, aren't we, Mama?"

"The Luray Caverns!" Aunt Sissy Two snorted. She was almost as good at that as Heaven, Iva thought. "My idea of fun isn't stumbling around a damp hole in the ground with two five-year-olds."

"Till death do us part," Lily Pearl told her sternly.

Aunt Sissy Two stared at Iva's mother. "What did she say?"

"Wedding vows. Lily Pearl memorized them," Arden said. "Where are we going?"

"Stingray Point," Iva's mother replied. "It's on the Chesapeake Bay. We leave day after tomorrow for the trip of a lifetime!"

"Yay!" Iva cried.

"Yay!" Heaven said. She hugged Iva. Iva hugged her back.

Stingray Point! The very name promised adventure and danger. For five whole days, Iva would become Iva Honeysuckle, Great Discoverer. She ran to the door, eager to pack her discovery shorts and pup tent.

"My Daily Life card was right," Heaven said smugly. "I am too going on a trip."

"So am I!"

"You're going on my trip. Don't take too much stuff, Iva. You're staying with me on the sleeping porch, and I hate to be crowded." Just like that, Heaven could flip back into her old self.

"And you leave those bottles of toilet water home. I don't want my porch stunk up!"

"I think I'll make a special Daily Life at the Beach card deck," Heaven said. "All the cards will have fun things to do. With other people."

"Fine!"

Iva slammed the screen door behind her, even though it wasn't her house. She didn't need Heaven's dumb old Daily Life cards to tell her what to do each day.

Iva knew exactly what she would do at Stingray Point. Find pirates' treasure.

Chapter Two

Stingray Point

"Captain John Smith discovered Stingray Point," Iva said from the front seat. She turned around to make sure Arden and Hunter didn't miss a word. "I read about him in the September 1939 issue of *National Geographic*. You can borrow it if you want."

"No, thanks," said Hunter.

"I also read about him in a library book. Captain John Smith discovered Jamestown. You remember, don't you, Mama, back when you were in school?"

"I seem to recall something along those lines," said her mother.

"Everybody was unhappy at Jamestown. They were starving and arguing."

"Starvation tends to make people grouchy,"

Arden said. She and Hunter were chewing bubble gum and drawing pictures of the bikinis they planned to wear when they met their imaginary boyfriend, Rory. Apparently, he was going to the beach, too.

Iva went on. "Captain John Smith took a bunch of men, and they sailed off. They were looking for food and gold for the starving colonists—"

"Yum! A gold sandwich," Hunter said, poking Arden. They laughed their new fake laugh, which sounded like a cross between a hiccuping donkey and squealing tires.

"Mama!" Iva complained. "Tell them to quit it."

Looking in the rearview mirror, Iva's mother made hard eyes at the girls in the backseat. "Do you two want to ride in the other car? Split up this time?"

"No, Mama."

"No, Aunt Sissy."

"Then let Iva talk."

Arden flung herself dramatically against the window. "But, Mama, Iva always tells these

boring old stories about boring old stuff."

"I do not!" Iva twisted around again. She had learned the fine art of making hard eyes herself.

"Arden, honey," their mother said, "you know Iva can't do anything without reading about it. It's her nature. Let her tell her story."

Iva resisted the urge to stick out her tongue at her sister and faced forward again. She might not have been the pretty older sister or the young cute one. She was the one who learned about things. That was why she called herself Iva Honeysuckle, Great Discoverer. She was her own self, not just a Honeycutt cousin or sister.

"Captain John Smith's men weren't very good about getting food. They tried to catch fish in a frying pan!" She giggled.

Her mother changed lanes to keep up with Aunt Sissy Two's car.

Arden began kicking the back of Iva's seat.

"Mama, Arden's kicking my seat!"

"Mama, Arden's kicking my seat," Arden said, mimicking her.

Flipping on her right blinker, Mrs. Honeycutt checked the traffic, then swung off the highway into a bank parking lot.

"Listen, girls. It's a long drive to Stingray Point, and everybody has to get along. That means you, too, Arden."

"We'd get along a whole lot better if Iva would be quiet," Arden said.

Iva was amazed. Her sister was really skating on thin ice.

In her you're-plucking-my-last-nerve tone, Mrs. Honeycutt said, "Arden, if you don't straighten up, I'll turn this car around and take you back. You can stay with your Uncle Buddy. He'd be tickled to have somebody fix his breakfast and pack his lunch."

Uncle Buddy, who worked nights at the box factory, was staying at Iva's house to take care of Sweetlips, her beagle. Iva's father, a long-distance trucker, was in Oregon.

Arden slumped in her seat. She didn't say a word. Neither did Hunter, even though she wasn't in trouble. As cousins and best friends, they stuck together.

"We've switched cars once already because Iva and Heaven were acting up," Mrs. Honeycutt reminded them.

Now Iva slumped in her seat. It was true. She and Heaven had begun squabbling before the car doors were shut.

Heaven had wanted to sit by the left window. She said the view was better. But Iva claimed that window. Heaven grumbled that Iva's *National Geographic* magazines took up too much of the room between them. Iva said nobody needed to bring daisy-embroidered bedsheets to the beach—they'd just get all sandy.

After fifteen minutes, Iva's mother pulled over and put Howard in the back with Iva. Heaven smirked, because now she got to be up front. The Queen's Seat, she called it. Iva said Heaven needed a seat all to herself, because her butt was so big.

At the next rest stop, Lily Pearl, Heaven, and

Howard were exchanged for Arden and Hunter. "Like prisoners of war," Arden had said bitterly. She and Hunter could get away with murder in Aunt Sissy Two's car.

"Well? What's it going to be?" Mrs. Honeycutt glared at Arden in so steely a manner that Iva wondered why the rearview mirror didn't shatter.

"I won't bother Iva anymore." But Arden flicked Iva a secret searing glance.

Their mother steered the car back onto the highway. "All right, then."

Iva picked up the thread of her story as if nothing had happened. "So, Captain John Smith sailed up this river that has two *p*'s and two *n*'s in its name. He took his sword and stabbed a stingray. The stingray stabbed his arm with its poisonous tail!"

With a sigh, Iva's mother followed Aunt Sissy Two into a gas station. "Lily Pearl must have to go again."

Iva didn't stop talking when they got out of

the car. As the middle kid in a family like hers, she had to make the best of every opportunity. "Captain John Smith got very, very sick. He almost died. He told his men to dig his grave. But then the doctor that was with them put some medicine on Captain John Smith's arm and he was cured. So from then on, the place was called Stingray Point. And that's where we're going!" Iva finished with a flourish.

"What happened to the grave?" Hunter asked, popping a bubble.

"Oh, my gosh! What's that smell?" Arden rolled her window down and stuck her head out like a golden retriever.

"Mmmm!" Hunter pushed Arden aside so she could hang out the window, too.

Iva sniffed. The aroma pouring through their windows suggested sugar and onions and tomatoes and really, really good meat. "Mama, what is it?" she asked.

"Just the finest open-pit barbecue chicken this

side of Jericho." Iva's mother slowed the car and followed Aunt Sissy Two's car onto a graveled lot. "Aunt Sissy Two and I used to go to Stingray Point with Mama and Pap when we were kids. Right about lunchtime we'd come to Critch Jackson's barbecue stand. That smell would draw us off the highway like a magnet."

Iva expected a restaurant, but she saw only two big, smoking barbecue pits and one African American man slapping a paintbrush over grilled chickens.

Before Mrs. Honeycutt had switched off the ignition, everyone piled out of the car and ran over to the grills. Lily Pearl and Howard and Heaven were close behind.

Iva was practically drooling. "Mama, can we get some?"

"You bet." Her mother ordered three quarter chickens and two drumsticks for Iva.

"Here you go, missy," the man said. He handed Iva a paper plate bending under the weight of the two huge charcoal-blackened drumsticks.

"How come the chickens aren't red?" Iva asked. "You know, like catsup?"

"I use a special white barbecue sauce," Mr. Jackson said. "Oil and vinegar and secret spices. My recipe goes all the way back to the first settlers."

"From Captain John Smith?" Iva said, thrilled to be eating real discoverer food.

"Maybe."

Iva noticed his gold front tooth winking in the sun. Back home, a friend had a chipped front tooth that Iva had always admired. Mr. Jackson's gold tooth was beautiful. She wondered how she could get one.

They sat down at a picnic table. Arden and Hunter ripped into their chickens like jungle cats. Howard stripped his drumstick to the bone in a jiffy. Even picky-picky Lily Pearl ate without talking.

Iva bit into the tangy meat. Sauce dripped down her chin. She had never tasted anything so wonderful in her entire life. Not even Walser Compton's angel food cake with peppermint icing could compare.

She looked around. Heaven, always the last to leave the table, was missing.

Heaven was talking to Critch Jackson as he slathered sauce on chickens. Lily Pearl and Howard slipped off the bench and raced over. Iva wasn't about to be left out.

Heaven showed Iva something in her hand. A flat copper disk lay on her palm.

"See this penny?" she said. "When Mr. Jackson was a little boy, he put the penny on the trolley-car tracks—did you know there used to be a trolley car in Stingray Point? Anyhow, the trolley car ran over it and squashed it flat." Sure enough, Abraham Lincoln's head was all stretched.

"Did you live in Stingray Point?" Iva asked Mr. Jackson.

"Grew up there."

"I read in my *National Geographic* magazine about pirates' lairs in the Chesapeake Bay. Did you ever find one?" Iva wasn't sure what a lair looked like.

Critch Jackson turned over a row of sizzling chickens. "Never found a pirate's lair. But one day out in my boat, I saw some puffin' pigs."

"What are they?" Howard asked.

"You'd call them porpoises," Mr. Jackson replied. "Very scarce animals. But that day, I had my lucky penny with me, and that's how I got to see them. A while back, people saw something else in the bay—they said it was a sea serpent."

Iva nearly fell over. "A sea serpent? Really?"

"That's what I heard. They said it was a great big thing. Named her Chessie."

Heaven, who had the imagination of a paper clip, ignored this fascinating story and asked, "What other lucky things did your penny do?"

"Almost spent that penny one time, buying a bucket of oysters. But I broke a five-dollar bill instead. When I opened one of them oysters, I found a pearl!"

"My name is Lily Pearl!" piped up Lily Pearl.

"You could have swallowed it," Iva said to Mr. Jackson. "The pearl, I mean."

"Lucky penny kept me from doing that, too," he said. "I had the pearl made into a necklace for my wife to wear on our wedding day."

Lily Pearl tugged on Mr. Jackson's shirtsleeve. "You had a wedding? Did your bride have a white dress and a long veil?"

Mr. Jackson nodded. "And the pearl necklace, which she never took off."

"From this day forward," Lily Pearl said solemnly.

"Kids!" called Aunt Sissy Two. "Come clean up your trash."

Iva wrinkled her nose with annoyance. She'd wanted to ask Mr. Jackson about pirates' lairs and a lot more about that sea serpent, but Lily Pearl had sidetracked him with her ridiculous bride talk.

At the garbage can, Heaven showed Iva the penny still in her hand. "Look what Mr. Jackson gave me." She smiled as if he'd presented her with the Hope Diamond.

Iva was suspicious. "How come he gave it to you?"

"Because I let him choose a card from my special Daily Life at the Beach deck. He was so excited he gave me his penny." Heaven polished the penny on the hem of her T-shirt. "I'm going to carry it with me always and have good luck."

"It's just a penny," Iva said. No wonder Heaven kept asking for lucky stories.

"You wish."

"He can't give stuff to you and not anybody else!" Iva said, raising her voice.

Mr. Jackson walked over to Aunt Sissy Two. "Your daughter asked for an old penny. I didn't mean to cause any hard feelings among the children."

"Heaven," said Aunt Sissy Two, "let Mr. Jackson have his penny back."

"No!" Heaven gripped the coin in her fist. "It's mine!"

Mr. Jackson looked as if he had a sudden headache. "How about I give all of you something?"

Iva's spirits lifted. Maybe he'd offer her something better than a flat penny—like a pocketknife.

But he said, "I'd like to pack you-all a nice picnic supper."

Iva's mother and Aunt Sissy Two tucked an envelope into Critch Jackson's money box. Iva figured they were leaving a tip, so he could buy himself a supersize headache remedy.

They all got back on the highway. In Iva's car, no one spoke. After a while, Iva smelled something else in the air. Not barbecued chicken, but the delicious odor of dead fish. Then a wide band of sparkling dark blue water filled the view.

The Chesapeake Bay.

"We're here!" she cried.

"Finally," her mother said with relief.

As they passed the metal sign that said, WELCOME TO STINGRAY POINT, Iva turned to her mother and asked, "If somebody hits me in the face with a humongous seashell and my front tooth falls out, can I get a gold one?"

Chapter Three

The Man Upstairs

The yellow two-story rental house looked crooked and rickety, like one of Lily Pearl's drawings. A rusty glider and some dingy wicker chairs crouched in the shade of the wide front porch. High up on the peaked roof, a heron-shaped weather vane creaked in the breeze.

Iva was enchanted.

"Our house has a name! Heron's Rest!" she exclaimed, pointing to the driftwood sign over the door. Then she dropped to her hands and knees as if she'd been struck by lightning. "The driveway is made out of oyster shells. They're probably millions of years old—"

"Iva, get up. You're embarrassing me." Arden sashayed past wearing pink sunglasses and a straw hat. Talk about embarrassing, Iva thought, imitating her sister's prissy walk up the porch steps and into the house.

In the kitchen, Iva's mother warily checked out the old-fashioned stove while Aunt Sissy Two announced room assignments.

"The bedroom at the end of the hall is Arden's and Hunter's. Lily Pearl will sleep on a cot with Aunt Sissy and me, because our room is closest to the bathroom."

Howard pushed back his sweaty bangs. "What about me?"

"You"—Aunt Sissy Two used her aren't-you-special voice—"get to sleep in the living room on the sofa!"

"Oh, boy! Can I watch TV all night?"

"There is no TV," Hunter said in disgust.

Heaven said, "Where's this sleeping porch I have to share with Iva?"

"Other side of the kitchen—"

Iva raced through the door onto a screened-in porch. The addition seemed to have been built by a chimpanzee. Nails stuck out all over the place, and the floor sloped down.

The half walls were painted battleship gray. A beat-up wooden chest squatted between two metal cots with skimpy rolled-up mattresses. At the other end of the porch, a modern leather rocking chair looked apologetic.

"This is it?" Heaven said, with fists on hips. "No curtains, no rug, no lamps—"

"It's not supposed to be the Ritz Hilton," Iva said. "I think it's neat. We can pretend we're camping out."

"What if it rains? Our beds are right by the screens. We'll get soaking wet!"

"See those plastic things above the windows? Blinds. Now, quit griping, and get your stuff so we can hit the beach."

Iva skipped out to the car and returned with her suitcase. Next, she carried in the box containing her earthly possessions—her pup tent, her old *National Geographic* magazines, her discoverer's journal that was really an old tire-pressure record book, and her corduroy discoverer's shorts.

She was happily stowing these items in the wooden chest when Heaven let out a shriek.

"What?" Iva jumped up, thinking there was a scorpion in the corner.

"We don't have a closet!"

Her cousin stood tragically in the doorway, surrounded by five small suitcases. Heaven had bought them cheap at Cazy Sparkle's yard sale.

"We're only here for five days," said Iva. "You only need one ball gown."

"Very funny," Heaven replied. "I brought one suitcase for each card in my Daily Life at the Beach deck."

"What are you babbling about?"

Heaven flopped down in the chair. "I made five Daily Life at the Beach cards, right? One for each day we're here. Each card has a different beach activity. I packed a different suitcase for each card. When I pull the card with that activity on it, I wear the stuff from that suitcase."

Iva stared at her. They were not related. They couldn't be. A Martian must have shoved Heaven Honeycutt out of a spaceship.

Unlike her cousin, Iva planned to wear the same outfit every single day. What's more, she wasn't going to take a bath or wash her hair or brush her teeth. Captain John Smith didn't take a bath for months.

"What if your Daily Life card says to look for shells that day, only we're in the middle of a hurricane?" Iva said. "What suitcase do you use then?"

Heaven kicked her ladies'-size flip-flops across the room and sniffed with her left nostril. "You think you know everything."

"I know those beach life cards are lame."

Heaven got up and jerked two of her suitcases over to the wooden chest. "You've filled it up already! What am I supposed to do with my things?"

"You snooze, you lose."

"We'll see about that!" Heaven reached in and began tossing out Iva's *National Geographics*.

"Hey," Iva yelled. "Those are rare antiques!"

To get even, she unlatched one of the suitcases and flung a red-striped shirt, some white shorts, and a navy windbreaker over her shoulder. "What's this, your beach-party outfit?"

At the bottom of the suitcase was a bottle of Pretty Peach cologne. Iva sprayed the mist all over Heaven.

"Stop it!" Heaven screeched, flailing her arms. "I'm telling!"

"What's going on?" Iva's mother stepped out

onto the porch, followed by Aunt Sissy Two. Both carried sheets, blankets, and pillows.

"Iva's being mean, Aunt Sissy!" Heaven said. "Look what she did to my clothes!"

"Look what *she* did to *my* stuff," Iva said quickly. With a champion tattletale like Heaven around, you had to get your licks in fast.

Mrs. Honeycutt glanced at the meager furniture. "Sissy, the kids don't have any storage. No closet. Not even a dresser. Just that chest."

"Which Iva has piled her stupid stuff in—"

"Heaven," said Aunt Sissy Two, "I told you not to bring all these suitcases. You snuck them in the trunk anyway, didn't you?"

"Mama, Iva sprayed my cologne in the air, wasting it," Heaven said in that Sunday-school tone she used when she didn't want to answer a question.

Mrs. Honeycutt dumped the sheets onto the chair and faced Iva and Heaven.

"Here's the deal, girls. If you can't get along, then one of you will switch with Lily Pearl and sleep in our room on the cot. The person who stays here gets to take Lily Pearl to the bathroom six times a night."

Iva looked at Heaven. Heaven looked at Iva.

"We'll stay," Iva said. She'd rather sleep on the porch, even if it meant being kept awake by Heaven's snoring all night.

"No more arguing?" Aunt Sissy Two said.

Heaven shook her head.

Iva spied her cousin's fingers crossed behind her back.

Then Heaven knelt by the chest and began stacking Iva's magazines just so.

The instant their mothers left, Heaven shoveled in the rest of Iva's belongings.

"Don't think you've won," she muttered.

But Iva was listening to her mother and Aunt Sissy Two talking in the kitchen.

"It'll never work, those two," her mother said. "Remember that time they were playing in the basement? We were painting the nursery before Lily Pearl was born."

"Yeah," said Aunt Sissy Two. "They must have been about four."

"They were playing good; then, all of a sudden, it got real quiet. I cracked the door, and there sat Heaven on the top step, with Iva on the bottom step. Both of them grumped up in a big bullfrog pout." Iva's mother sighed. "All they ever do is fall out."

Iva remembered that time. Heaven had quit a perfectly fun game of orphans-lost-in-the-graveyard because she wanted to play ice princesses instead.

"Which bed do you want, Iva?" Heaven asked sweetly, directing her voice toward the kitchen.

"Which one do you want?" Iva asked, suspecting a trap.

"Doesn't matter to me." Heaven shook out her daisy-embroidered sheets with an expert snap.

Iva often thought her cousin should have had her own TV show. "Then I'll take this one." She unrolled the mattress of the bed closest to the screen. She'd be able to smell the sea air a second sooner than Heaven would.

When Heaven unrolled her mattress, she yelled like she'd struck oil. "Look what I found!" She held up a pretty shell with orangey-pink insides.

"That was in your bed?" Iva said enviously.

"Yep. Lucky for me I picked this bed." Heaven set the shell on the chest.

"Luck has nothing to do with it." But Iva was wondering what she'd find in her bed. "You got the bed I didn't want."

"Exactly," said Heaven.

Arden and Hunter skidded out onto the porch. "Hurry up!" Arden said. "We're going to the beach!"

"The beach! The beach! The beach!" Lily Pearl and Howard cried, hopping like sand fleas. Lily Pearl strutted in her brand-new blue satin two-piece bathing suit.

"Wait till I make my bed first—"

"Heaven!" Iva wasn't even taking her discovery notebook.

They stampeded through the kitchen and into the living room like water buffalo. Iva's mother and Aunt Sissy Two stood on either side of the front door.

"Not so fast," said Aunt Sissy Two. "Rule time."

"Can we hear them later?" Arden said. "Me and Hunter are in kind of a hurry."

"Number one," Iva's mother said crisply. "The most important rule of all. Lily Pearl and Howard must be watched at all times. This means in the yard, on the beach, on the boardwalk."

Arden slumped so that one hip jutted out. "And who gets stuck with the little kids? Me and Hunter, that's who. Some vacation this is going to be."

"Arden . . ."

"It's true, Mama! Iva never does a stroke of work. It's always me watching Lily Pearl!"

Lily Pearl danced in her blue bathing suit, delighted to be the subject of so much drama.

Aunt Sissy Two said, "Iva and Heaven will watch them, too. Heaven is very responsible."

Iva's mother looked doubtfully at Aunt Sissy Two. "I don't know. Iva is kind of reckless. Somebody may need to watch after her."

"Hey!" Iva said, insulted.

Good old responsible Heaven just smiled.

"Rule number two," Aunt Sissy Two said. "No one goes in the water unless one of us is on the beach."

Iva's mother said, "You'll each have five dollars to spend this week for souvenirs—"

"Can I have mine now?" Arden asked eagerly.

"Tomorrow. If you blow it all in one day, too bad. And no trading nickels for quarters with Lily Pearl and Howard or 'borrowing' from them," said Mrs. Honeycutt. "That's rule number three."

Iva planned to save her money until the very last day. She would go to all the gift shops and look at every single thing before she spent her five dollars.

"Is that all?" Hunter asked anxiously.

Iva figured Arden and Hunter had an imaginary

date with Rory. Since he was an imaginary boy-friend, he shouldn't mind if they were late.

Suddenly, there was a thumping sound over-head. Iva had been so excited about the sleeping porch, she had completely forgotten the house had a second story.

"What's that noise?" she asked.

"The second floor is rented to a gentleman," Aunt Sissy Two replied. She glanced at Iva's mother. "Little does he know."

Iva looked around for a staircase. "How does he get up there?"

Her mother pointed to a door near the sofa. "The stairs are on the other side of that door. The rental lady said he keeps unusual hours and we'll probably never see him come and go."

Unusual hours. What did that mean? Iva was intrigued. "Is it okay—"

Her mother cut her off. "Rule number four. Do not go upstairs into that man's room. Under-stand?" Her gaze rested on Iva.

"The beach!" Howard yelled.

"I now pronounce you wife and husband!" Lily Pearl shouted.

Iva burst out the door with the others.

"No one puts a toenail in the water till we get there!" Aunt Sissy Two hollered over the porch rail. "We'll be down in fifteen minutes."

Iva stopped in the oyster-shell driveway and turned to glance back at the second-story windows.

Now she had two assignments. One, find pirates' treasure. And two, find out about The Man Upstairs.

Chapter Four

London Howdyshell

Iva ran like sixty across the scorching beach. People frowned as she kicked sand onto their towels. Seagulls preening on the rock jetty flew up like popcorn.

Little waves rimmed with spitty foam curled on the hard-packed sand. Iva stopped at the water's edge and let the waves cool her burning feet.

She gazed at the horizon and imagined she was one of Captain John Smith's crew. They had just landed in this new place. Not another person nor even a wild animal in sight, only wilderness, teeming with bears and wolves—

"The notion!" Lily Pearl shrieked behind her. "Iva's swimming in the *notion*!"

"It's not the *notion*," Iva told her. "It's the *ocean*, and do I look like I'm swimming?"

Lily Pearl and Howard squatted down and began digging in the wet sand. Arden and Hunter halted by the lifeguard tower to gawk at the tanned blond lifeguard. They stood motionless, mouths slack, as if they'd been stunned by a ray gun.

Last came Heaven. She slogged toward Iva, her big feet spewing sand like walrus flippers. "You broke rule number two. Nobody is supposed to go in the water unless our mothers are here."

"I didn't go in the water," Iva said truthfully. "The water got on me." She splashed Heaven's legs. "There. Now you broke the rule, too."

Lily Pearl piled sand around Howard's ankles. "We wanna swim in the notion."

"It's the bay, not the ocean," Iva corrected. "It goes all the way to Maryland. Isn't it great here? I never want to go home."

Heaven wiped the water off her legs, like it was evidence at a crime scene. "It's too hot."

"It's supposed to be hot. It's the beach. Discoverers are used to being out in all weathers."

Iva puffed out her chest, as if daring the skies to hurl hailstones, snowballs, and lightning bolts at her.

"Don't you know everything in the world has already been found?" Heaven said.

"Has not!"

"Has too. Face it, Iva. People in your line of work are hard up. You need to go to Saturn or someplace to find anything new."

"I'm gonna send *you* to Saturn." But Iva's threat lacked passion. Much as she hated to admit it, her cousin might have been right.

Explorers these days didn't have it easy like Captain John Smith. Four hundred years ago, he'd tooled up and down the Chesapeake Bay and that river with two *p*'s and two *n*'s, discovering creeks and points and islands left and right. It wasn't fair.

"You wait. I'm gonna find a creek or an animal or—a rock that nobody else has found!" Iva didn't want Heaven to know she planned to find pirates' treasure.

"I could discover a rock." Heaven walked over to the jetty and sat on a boulder half buried in the sand. "I dub thee the Heaven Rock."

"Discoverers don't say that 'dub thee' stuff," Iva sneered. She hopped up on the flattish stone to get a better look around. Maybe Captain John Smith had left behind an old sword or something.

"Get off my rock," Heaven said.

"Possession is nine-tenths of the law," Iva tossed back. "I bet that's what Captain John Smith said when he came here."

"Actually," said a voice on the other side of the jetty, "he probably went, 'Ouch!'"

Iva looked down. A girl her age was hunkered down at the water's edge. As she grinned up at Iva, her straight black hair swung out like a crow's wing. She wore some sort of rock on a chain around her neck.

"You know about Captain John Smith!" Iva cried. In her excitement, she leaped off the boulder, landing with a jolt that jarred her teeth.

"You okay?" the black-haired girl asked.

Iva brushed sand off her shins. "Yeah."

Heaven's large shadow stretched over them. "Don't worry about Iva. One time she jumped off the shed roof with a paper bag in each hand. Trying to fly."

"And I did, for a split second." Leave it to Heaven to give the new girl the wrong impression about her. "I'm Iva. We just got here today. This is Heaven. We're distantly related."

Heaven glared at her.

"Hi. I'm London Howdyshell."

Iva was instantly struck by name envy. London Howdyshell sounded like somebody important. Maybe a TV newsperson. *This is London Howdyshell, reporting from the Belgian Congo.*

London flipped her hair back. Tiny diamond earrings sparkled in the sun.

"Are those real?" Heaven demanded. "How much did they cost?"

"No idea," London replied. "I've been wearing them since I was three."

She scooped up a wire strainer of sand and sifted it over a plastic bucket.

"How come you're playing in the sand like a little kid?" Heaven asked.

"I'm looking for fossil sharks' teeth." London shook a baby-food jar with three tiny, triangular teeth.

"Can I see?" Iva took the jar. "Wow, these are really cool."

"The teeth are from the Miocene period. From a bull shark. I want to find a tiger shark tooth. Morning is better, because the tide's low."

London Howdyshell sounded like a regular scientist. Scientists and discoverers often teamed up together. Iva had just made her first discovery—a beach friend!

In her *National Geographic* explorer voice, Iva said, "Captain John Smith almost died in this very spot. I'm going to look for the stingray skeleton that stung him."

"Stingrays don't have skeletons," London informed her. "Like sharks don't. Anyway, Smith ate that stingray for supper that night."

"Ewww," said Heaven.

Iva sat back on her heels. She hadn't known that. And she knew everything about Captain John Smith and Stingray Point. At least, she thought she did.

"Are you sure?" she asked.

"Not only that," London went on matter-of-factly, "most people think Smith's doctor rubbed ointment on his arm to make it better. But what really happened was that a Native American put mud from Antipoison Creek on it. That's what saved him."

"Where's Antipoison Creek?" Iva asked. It sounded like a neat place.

"Off the Rappahannock River." London knew about that river with the two *p*'s and two *n*'s! They had so much in common!

Lily Pearl and Howard came running over. They stared at London in awe.

"I like your necklace," Lily Pearl said to London. "Where did you buy it?"

"I made it myself," London replied. "I found the rock on this beach."

"Are you from this country?" asked Howard.

"You kids are weird. Yes, I'm American. Part Greek, part Italian, part French, and part Scottish. But I've lived in other countries. We just moved from Singapore."

"You lived in Singapore?" Heaven asked.

"And Germany and Australia and California. My dad's in the navy."

Iva was flooded with admiration. London had been all over the globe! She didn't want this cool girl to think she, Iva, was a plain old nobody.

"I'm a bunch of parts, too," she announced. "Part English, part Cherokee, and—part Irish setter."

London laughed. "An Irish setter is a dog."

"And we are not part Cherokee," Heaven put in. "We have exactly the same relatives on both sides."

"Don't remind me." Iva squinted at her cousin. If only she could ditch Heaven so she and London could hang out like real discoverers. But Heaven stood in front of them, legs apart, solid as the lifeguard stand.

"Here comes our mamas," Lily Pearl shrieked, racing Howard up the beach.

"We have to go," Iva told London. "Are you just here for the day?"

"My dad's friend is letting us stay in his house for three whole weeks," she replied. "It's only our second week."

"Then we'll see you around," Iva said, matching London's casual tone.

"Isn't she smart?" Heaven said to Iva as they plowed through the sand. "I've never met anybody that smart. And she has real diamond earrings."

But Iva was busy thinking. She'd finally met the girl she was supposed to be best-best friends with. Best of all, they weren't related!

After supper, they all rambled up Bayview Avenue. Clouds like scatter rugs drifted over the bay. Iva caught sight of the boardwalk—a covered walkway lined with restaurants, food stalls, and gift shops—and streaked ahead.

"Get back here!" her mother yelled. Iva marched back to the others. "Iva, would you keep an eye on Lily Pearl tonight? Heaven, will you watch Howard?"

"We're free!" Arden and Hunter sang, heading for the shops.

"If you spend your souvenir money tonight," Aunt Sissy Two warned them, "you don't get any more."

"What about ice cream and stuff?" Hunter asked. "Do we have to spend our money on that? It'll never last!"

"We'll spring for food," her mother replied.

There was a lot to see, but Iva felt chained to Lily Pearl, who minced along wearing that stupid lace curtain on her head. "Come on, Lily Pearl!"

"Brides have to walk slow," Lily Pearl said.

Iva jerked her into the gift shop. Howard obediently followed Heaven up and down the aisles. Lucky Heaven, Iva thought, assigned to a normal kid.

Arden was trying on a pair of red sunglasses with colored stones. "What do you think?" she asked Hunter.

"You look divine." Hunter held up a pair of purple sandals. "Gorgeous, huh?"

"Okay, I'll buy the sunglasses. You get those purple sandals. We can swap."

"You shouldn't spend your money the first night," Heaven told them. "I'm not."

"That's because you're tighter than the skin on a grape," Hunter said as she and Arden paid for their purchases.

"Hee-hee," Iva said. Heaven scowled at her, but it was the truth. Heaven rarely parted with a dime unless it was at Cazy Sparkle's yard sales.

Back on the boardwalk, Iva spotted a tanned blond boy talking to a guy with a camera. "Hey, isn't that blond guy the lifeguard?"

"It is!" Arden gasped so hard Iva was surprised all the sand on the beach didn't swirl up in a giant sandstorm.

The photographer snapped a couple's picture, then gave them a ticket. "Gotta get busy. See you later, Mike." He went away, and the blond guy moved on, too.

"His name is Mike!" Arden squealed, so shrilly that sled dogs in Anchorage could hear her. She grasped Hunter's elbows and they jumped up and down.

"Hey, there's London!" Heaven said.

London Howdyshell was strolling with her parents, licking a triple-scoop frozen-custard cone.

Heaven waved like she was on the deck of a cruise ship. "London! Over here!"

Iva frowned. London was *her* friend. *She* should have called her.

London sauntered over. "You should try the frozen custard."

"Can I?" Iva asked her mother. "A triple-decker cone like London's?"

"Two scoops," her mother said. "Get Lily Pearl a single-dip cone."

Iva dragged Lily Pearl over to the frozen custard stand. "Vanilla and chocolate cone. Big scoops. With sprinkles."

"I'll have the same," Heaven ordered. "Please." She gave Iva a look.

Arden and Hunter split a hot-fudge sundae. Lily Pearl and Howard each got a small cone.

"Eat your custard before it runs away," Iva's mother told Lily Pearl and Howard.

Lily Pearl put two fingers under the point of her cone. "Mine is running away!"

The mothers sat on a bench. Iva and the others dashed in and out of the gift shops. London joined them. She pointed to a restaurant called the Crab Shack.

"We eat there every night. The crab cakes are excellent," she said with the authority of someone who'd been at Stingray Point a whole week already. "You're a slow eater," she said to Iva. "Bet I finish my cone first, and I have three whole scoops."

"Bet you don't." Iva began licking furiously. An ice-cream-finishing contest! Heaven would never bolt her food. This was the perfect way to show London how much she and Iva had in common.

Iva ate so fast a sharp pain stabbed her temple. She gobbled her ice cream in great, throat-freezing gulps. Her cone was half gone when she heard a familiar cry.

Lily Pearl! Where was she?

Her little sister stood just inside the doorway of the Beach Shop. Iva hurried across the boardwalk.

"I was just making the scarfs go around like butterflies," Lily Pearl said defensively.

Her ice-cream cone was stuck in one of those spinning displays of silk scarves. Vanilla smeared every single scarf on the rack. They were all ruined.

Iva glanced across the boardwalk. London and Heaven were talking. And Howard—the good little kid—was sitting quietly beside them. Lucky Heaven.

"My cone," Lily Pearl whimpered. "Iva, get it out."

"I can't." Iva hoped the clerk wouldn't notice them. How much would all those scarves cost? "We have to leave it."

"I want my cone!" Lily Pearl opened her mouth and let loose a wail like a firehouse siren.

"Shh!" Iva pushed her out of the store. There was only one way to make her sister be quiet. She gave Lily Pearl her own cone.

London came over with Heaven. "I won," she said, brandishing the nubbin of her cone.

Heaven said to Iva, "You broke rule number one. You didn't watch Lily Pearl."

"So, tell on me. You're two tattles behind."

"Maybe I will. Maybe I won't." Heaven linked arms with London and they ambled down the boardwalk.

Iva couldn't believe it. Just like that, Heaven had swooped down on London Howdyshell. But their friendship wouldn't last. Heaven had nothing in common with London.

She trudged along with Lily Pearl, who licked Iva's cone very, very slowly. Little bitty licks, she told Iva, the way a bride would eat ice cream on her wedding day.

Chapter Five

Chessie

"This house is a teetotal wreck," Iva's mother declared. "Girls, straighten up. And sweep. There's more sand in here than the Gobi Desert." Then she and Aunt Sissy Two and the little kids zipped off to the farm stand, leaving Arden in dubious charge.

"Iva, do the dishes," Arden said. "Heaven, you sweep the floors."

To Iva, a vacation meant a break from doing chores she had to do at home. "What're you gonna do?"

"Supervise." Then Arden barricaded herself in the bathroom for her forty-seventh shower. When she came out, Hunter hurled herself in to take her shower.

"When are we supposed to use the bathroom?"

Heaven grumbled, pushing the broom over Iva's feet.

"I don't know why they have to take showers this morning anyway," Iva said. "We're going swimming later."

"That doesn't count. The water is all salty."

That didn't bother Iva. She was taking a vacation from being clean. The way she saw it, she was doing the environment a favor. Arden and Hunter had already taken so many showers it was a wonder the water level of the bay didn't drop, leaving the poor fish stranded.

Last night, before she went to bed, Iva fixed her hair in two pigtails. If she wore her hair the same way every day, no one would notice she never washed it. And she simply wet her toothbrush and put it back in the cup.

Arden shuffled in and plunked herself down at the kitchen table with a bottle of pink nail polish. She propped her foot up on an empty chair and began painting her toenails.

Heaven hung the broom on the rack. "Iva, you didn't make your bed."

"What're you? The bed police? I did so make it."

"You just slung the sheet up over your pajamas and a bunch of those moldy old magazines." Heaven snorted righteously through one nostril. "That is not making your bed."

Hunter came in, sat down, and put her foot on Arden's knee. "Do me."

The front door banged shut, making them all turn toward the living room.

"They can't be back yet," Iva said.

Arden, who could see the living room best, said, "It's that guy staying upstairs. He went out."

The Man Upstairs! Iva flew to the living room window but didn't see anyone. The plain black car that belonged to him was still parked on his side of the driveway. The tires were muddy, and she spotted a bunch of maps on the dashboard.

"I wonder who he is," she said. "I've never seen him."

"Maybe he's a movie star, hiding from his fans," Hunter said, bracing her other foot against Arden's knee.

"Why would a movie star hide at Stingray Point?" Arden argued. "It's hardly the Bahamas or anything. I bet he's a spy."

Iva looked back at his car. Then it hit her. The maps, the mud. It all fit! The Man Upstairs must be an explorer. He was probably on his way right now to do some serious exploring. If only she could talk to him! Maybe get some tips.

Then she heard the clang of a garbage-can lid. "He took his trash out!" she cried.

"Call National Security!" said Arden. She and Hunter cracked up.

Iva raced through the kitchen and out the back door, clattering down the wooden stairs. No one was on the sidewalk by the garbage cans. Iva checked the snowball bushes growing under the windows of their house. Not there, either.

A cottage had been built on the tiny lot behind their sleeping porch. The cottage had a separate oyster-shell driveway that led to Bayview Avenue. Iva ran down the driveway but saw no one on the street. Where had he gone? How had he gotten away so fast?

Then she stared at the garbage cans. How could she have overlooked the best source of information? She tossed the lid of the first can onto the ground and began pawing through the trash. Eggshells, Cheerios, coffee grounds, toast rinds. This was their can.

The second can had only one small bag, at the bottom. She pulled it out and dumped the contents onto the ground. Six Styrofoam coffee cups tumbled out. And some coffee-stained papers.

Kneeling, Iva spread the papers across the sidewalk. One was an envelope. The stains partly covered the first name, but she could read the last name: Smith.

She nearly keeled over. Smith! The Man Upstairs must be related to Captain John Smith, a great-great-great-great-great . . . Iva lost track of the greats. Now she knew Mr. Smith was an

explorer. He had followed his great-great-great-great-great-whatever John Smith's footsteps. It was in his blood. Just like it was in hers. They had so much in common!

Then she examined the other papers. Most were too stained to read. Iva frowned. Mr. Smith should have stuck to Kool-Aid. You could see through Kool-Aid spills.

She smoothed the last paper. It was partly stained, but she could read most of it:

You will locate 10 sites spaced no closer than 0.5 mile apart.

Each site will be geographically sequential.

You will try to locate [stain]
You will avoid dangerous [stain]
You will avoid private prop—[stain]
You will establish your route in the daytime, but following your route at night will be still be difficult.

Iva sucked in a breath. She was right! The paper proved it. Mr. Smith was some sort of explorer. And although Iva would never have admitted it in a million years, Arden was right, too. Mr. Smith was also a spy. He was . . . an explorer-spy!

This was huge. And nobody but Iva knew about it.

A car crunched up the cottage's driveway. Two old ladies climbed out, hauling suitcases. One of them spotted Iva crouching over the trash strewn all over the sidewalk.

"I hope you're going to pick up that mess, young lady," she said crisply. "We're here to relax, and we don't want to be bothered with a bunch of rowdy children."

Then you picked the wrong place to stay, Iva thought. She hurriedly gathered up the trash. But she put the piece of paper with Mr. Smith's instructions on it in her pocket.

"Sunscreen, camera, towels, books, snacks . . ." Iva's mother sorted through the contents of her straw tote.

"Can we go?" Dressed in her blue bathing suit, Lily Pearl swung her little plastic bag of beach toys. Howard waited patiently with his pail and shovel.

"We're waiting on Heaven," said Aunt Sissy Two, hefting the cooler of drinks. "Usually it's the big girls holding us up."

Arden and Hunter pranced at the front door like racehorses at the starting gate. They had brushed their hair until it crackled with static electricity, and they had checked to make sure they didn't have tuna fish between their teeth.

The sleeping-porch door opened, and out waltzed Heaven. She wore cutoffs, a T-shirt with a pink seashell on it, and very large, blindingly white tennis shoes.

"Hey, thanks for getting me a rowboat, too," Iva snickered.

"Very funny. Today's Daily Life at the Beach card is 'Shell Collecting,'" Heaven explained as they left the house. "This is my beachcombing outfit."

"I don't want to be seen with you." Iva walked behind the group.

On the beach, Arden and Hunter spread their towels directly in front of the lifeguard station. Then they lay down. Their pink toenails glittered in the sun.

"Miss," said Mike, the lifeguard, "you-all have to move. If I get a call, I'll need a clear path."

"Oh, of course," Arden said. She and Hunter dragged their towels a micrometer over to the right.

"Girls, did you put on sunscreen?" Aunt Sissy Two asked them.

"Yes," said Hunter. Iva knew she was fibbing.

She'd heard them plotting to get tans. Iva wasn't about to rat on them, since she hadn't had a bath in two days.

She marched past her mother and aunt's blanket, past the hole Howard and Lily Pearl had started digging in the sand, and down to the water's edge. Armed with a tea strainer from the beach house, she was eager to collect sharks' teeth.

London and Heaven were already stooped over a heap of shells. Iva joined them.

"London's found nine sharks' teeth already," Heaven said, as if London had stumbled on a pirates' chest of sapphires.

"Bet I find twenty-five," Iva said. She needed to impress London so she could pry her away from Heaven.

"Do you know what they look like?" London asked.

"Of course." Iva scraped the tea strainer in the sand and sifted. Something black glistened at the bottom of the mesh. "Found one already!"

London peered into the strainer. "That's part of a shell."

"Oh." Iva dumped it out and scooped more sand. "Here's one!"

"That's a shell, too," London informed her. "Broken shells look like sharks' teeth, because they're worn smooth. The tooth has three points. And it's a lighter color at the bottom."

Iva scooped and scooped. She found fingernail-size clamshells and mussel shells and chalky bits of oyster shells. But no sharks' teeth.

"Heaven," she whispered, "help me look."

"I don't have anything to put sand in," Heaven replied loudly. "I suppose I could use one of my rowboats—"

Iva was desperate. "I didn't mean that crack about your shoes. C'mon. We're family. We should stick together."

"We're family when it suits you." Heaven scooped wet sand with one hand and picked through the pile with her fingers. Then she snorted so hard she choked. A shiny black tooth nearly an inch long lay on her palm.

Iva stared at it. She'd been digging in that very spot!

London reached for the tooth. "A tiger shark's tooth! And it's a beauty! Lucky you." She gave the tooth back to Heaven.

"I am lucky," Heaven said, pulling the squashed penny from the pocket of her cutoffs. "Ever since Mr. Jackson gave me this I've been lucky as anything."

"I've always wanted a tiger shark's tooth," London said wistfully.

Heaven handed the tooth to London. "Then you keep it. You should have it."

"Really? Heaven, you're the best!" London squealed.

Iva felt a sour taste in the back of her throat. For the last two days, Heaven had been drawing good luck like a magnet. And now she had drawn London to her, too. It was hard to ignore the power of that lucky penny.

She got up and headed toward the fishing

pier. Let lucky old Heaven and her new friend London play in the sand. She had more important things to do. Like discovering.

There wasn't much to discover at the end of the pier. An old man was packing up his fishing tackle. Seagulls circled, hoping he'd throw them some leftover bait.

Iva shielded her eyes and gazed out into the bay. Choppy whitecaps hypnotized her. Up and down. Up and down. Shadows darted among the gray-green ripples.

She thought she saw a dark gray snakelike shape rise from the water. A second loop surfaced not too far away.

"Hey, mister," she said to the fisherman. "Are there porpoises here? I think I saw a couple." But when she pointed, the dark gray shapes were gone.

He looked in her direction. "Sometimes they play around the pier."

"What I saw looked like this." She sketched the loops in the air. "Only longer."

"You sure?"

She nodded.

"Porpoises are short and stubby. Sometimes people mistake them for dolphins, but dolphins have a longer snout."

"I didn't see any snout," Iva said. "Whatever it was, it was real big."

The man chuckled. "Maybe you saw Chessie."

The sea serpent Critch Jackson had talked about! It was supposed to live in the Chesapeake Bay!

Iva almost sprained her neck whipping her head toward the water. "Have you ever seen it?"

"Naw. I wasn't even around back when she was first spotted. People saw her a few years after that. Don't know as I believe in that stuff, but it makes a good story."

Iva tingled all over. She had just seen a sea monster! She was sure of it! Let London and Heaven have their dumb old sharks' teeth. She had made a valuable discovery. Probably even better than Mr. Smith, the explorer-spy, had ever made.

"I'm gonna be famous," she said, "because I just saw her!"

"If you want to say you saw Chessie," the man told her, "you need proof."

"What kind of proof?" Iva imagined herself trapping the huge sea monster in a net and hauling her to shore.

"A photograph. There's only one old picture of her, and it's real fuzzy."

"My mother has a camera!" Iva wasted no time. She pounded back down the pier and tore across the beach.

Luckily, her mother and Aunt Sissy Two were helping Howard and Lily Pearl dig their hole in the sand. Iva knew her mother wasn't likely to hand over her camera, not even to let Iva take a picture of a rare sea monster.

She slid the camera out of her mother's straw bag without being seen and plowed sand as she ran back to the pier. The fisherman was still there.

"Did she come up again?" Iva asked breathlessly.

"Nope. And I been keeping an eye out." He bent to fasten his tackle box.

Iva gazed unblinkingly out at the up-and-down water, willing Chessie to show herself again. She stared into the brightness until her eyes hurt.

After a minute or so, she spotted something

gray bobbing in the water. Was that Chessie's head breaking that ripply wave?

"Look!" she cried. "It's her again!"

"Where?" The fisherman leaned over the rail.

"There! See her?"

"That looks more like—"

Iva had to get this picture. She braced herself against the rail, squinting through the viewfinder. She jerked the button so hard the camera slipped from her hands.

"—A herring gull," the fisherman said. "They like to ride the waves."

Iva watched in horror as her mother's camera fell down, down into the green bay below. It plunged beneath the surface. And was gone forever.

Chapter Six

The Love Teller

Iva trailed behind her family as they went down the boardwalk. She was in no mood to browse for souvenirs or eat ice cream. She didn't even make fun of Heaven, who tripped along in a sundress and flowered sandals—her "boardwalk outfit."

Iva kept replaying the afternoon in her head. She had seen a sea monster! Twice! Okay, the second time was really a fat seagull pretending to be Chessie, but Chessie could have just been underneath the water.

No one would believe her, because she couldn't prove it. Even if she'd spotted twenty sea monsters and taken a picture good enough for the cover of *National Geographic*, her mother's camera lay at the bottom of the Chesapeake Bay.

Just before they left the beach house, Mrs. Honeycutt had searched her straw bag. "I thought I put my camera in here this morning," she said. "But I don't see it."

"It's somewhere in this hog-pen of a house," Aunt Sissy Two had said. "You'll find it."

Only if Mama has scuba-diving equipment, Iva thought now.

"There's Mike!" Arden shrieked to Hunter, pointing at the lifeguard by the Crab Shack. "Act grown-up so he'll notice us!"

She laughed her new fake laugh, startling a flock of robins from a tree. Then she shoved Hunter off the boardwalk.

Mike glanced over at them, then turned away instantly, as if from a car wreck.

The little kids were on fire to spend their souvenir money. Iva followed everyone into the Beach Shop. Clutching his five-dollar bill, Howard made a beeline for a tank filled with hermit crabs.

"Mama," he said. "Can I have one? I'm not sneezing." Howard was allergic to everything but oxygen. Heaven's cat, Yard Sale, had to live with Miz Compton, the Sunday-school teacher.

Aunt Sissy Two studied the spidery crabs poking out of their shells. "I guess."

A gum-chewing clerk put Howard's crab in a plastic cage and told him how to care for his pet. "His name is Hermy," Howard told her happily.

"Me next. I'm after something bride-ish," Lily Pearl said, sailing up and down the aisles. She braked suddenly by the jewelry counter and screamed.

Iva, who had drawn Lily Pearl duty again, ran over, afraid she'd cut herself or something.

Lily Pearl stood stock-still, her hands clasped near her mouth as she goggled at a silver chain with a single pearl. The sign read, PEARL NECKLACE. $19.50.

"I can read one of those words!" she said. "It says, *pearl*. That's a pearl, isn't it? Like the one Mr. Jackson found? The bride necklace is the perfect snooveneer."

"Very pretty," Iva said. "Except it costs nineteen

dollars and fifty cents, plus tax. You only have five dollars."

Lily Pearl's mouth squared and Iva knew what was coming.

"No use bawling. You don't have enough money. Period."

The dam burst anyway. "Dearly beloved! I want the bride necklace!"

Iva pulled her sobbing sister out of the store. Her mother and Aunt Sissy Two and Howard were sitting on the bench outside with Howard's new pet.

Lily Pearl threw herself at her mother's shoulder and cried as though her heart were breaking.

"Iva, leave her with me," her mother said, patting Lily Pearl's back. "The others are in the arcade. Here's a dollar."

The arcade was crowded with kids. Arden and Hunter were playing a car-driving machine. And Heaven was talking to—surprise, surprise—London Howdyshell.

Ignoring them, Iva cruised the machines.

Skee-Ball had the best prizes. Gigantic stuffed turquoise gorillas. Hats with propellers. And— Iva's blood stopped circulating for a beat—a fancy camera. Almost exactly like her mother's.

If she won the camera, she could slip it into her mother's straw tote under a towel or something. Her mother wouldn't know the difference.

London sidled up. "I'm good at this game. Want to see who gets the highest score?"

Iva lit up like a pinball machine. London must still want to be friends! Plus, the challenge was just what Iva needed. If she played against somebody, she'd win the camera for sure.

"You're on." She bought a dollar's worth of tokens, enough for one game.

"I want to play, too." Heaven jingled tokens in her sundress pocket.

They chose three Skee-Ball machines that were together in a row and dropped their tokens in. Iva pulled the lever on her machine. Nine wooden balls rolled from the chute.

"You want to roll your balls over the bumper

and into the rings with the highest number," London said. "The counter adds your score."

Iva could see this wouldn't be easy. The ramp inclined steeply upward. A net over the alley kept a person from simply throwing the ball into the rings.

Heaven went first. Her first ball wobbled up the ramp but bounced off the bumper. "London, what am I doing wrong?"

"Use your wrist," London told her. "Make the ball hop over."

"No fair giving hints." Iva went next. Her ball skipped over the ten-point ring and landed in the twenty-point ring. "Your turn."

London rolled her ball powerfully up into the thirty-point ring. Heaven scored a thirty-pointer, too. "Yay!" she cried, hopping up and down.

Rattled, Iva couldn't get her next four balls over the first bumper. The counter on London's machine racked up more points. Even Heaven was doing better than Iva.

Iva had one ball left. She needed to get it in the fifty-point ring, at the very top of the ramp. She took a final look at the camera on the prize shelf, then rolled the ball. It shot up, bouncing off the rims of the rings.

"Go! Go!" Iva yelled, punching her fist in the air.

The ball glanced off the rim of the fifty-pointer and banked off the side of the alley. It came to rest pathetically at the very bottom. No points.

London had one ball left, too. She took aim at the fifty-pointer. Miss, miss, Iva thought, hoping to jinx London's throw. London's ball flew up, hit the net, and slipped neatly into the fifty-pointer. Game over.

The scores lit up. Heaven had earned seventy points. She picked out a stuffed cat that, she said, looked just like Yard Sale. London claimed one of the gigantic turquoise gorillas. It was so big she couldn't even carry it.

Iva, who had the lowest score, received the "house" prize, a cheap plastic Frisbee.

"London's the expert Skee-Ball player of all time!" Heaven said, rubbing her stuffed cat against her cheek.

London blew on her knuckles and buffed them on her shirt.

"So I lost," Iva said. There was still one way to win London over. "I saw something today. Something real big. Bigger than that shark's tooth Heaven found."

"What?" London asked in an offhand way.

"Don't get her started," Heaven said. "Iva likes to make a mountain out of a molehill."

"I do not! Just for that I'm not going to tell you about the sea monster I saw!"

Heaven and London began laughing so hard they had to hold each other up.

"Honestly, Iva," Heaven said when she could

speak again. "How pathetic can you get? You're just no match for London."

Iva stalked to the other side of the arcade. She shouldn't have told them about Chessie yet. She should have waited until she had proof.

Arden and Hunter were playing a tall red metal machine with lights around a large dial. THE LOVE TELLER, OR, HOW TO GET A DATE was written in gold at the top.

"Give me a good answer!" Arden dropped a token into the coin slot. Lights chased around the dial and stopped on Spruce Up.

Iva broke up. "Guess you'll have to take more showers to get a date."

"My turn." Hunter's light stopped on Act Desperate. She pounded the machine.

"I don't want to act desperate around Mike."

Iva thought they were both desperate. "Poor old Rory," she said. "Does he know you're googly-eyed over the lifeguard?"

"Don't you have anything better to do?" Arden asked Iva.

Actually, she didn't. She went outside and sat on the bench. Lily Pearl's face was streaked with tears and chocolate ice cream.

"Here," Iva said. "I won this for you." She gave her sister the Frisbee.

Lily Pearl threw it across the boardwalk. "Don't want it! I want the bride necklace!"

"I think somebody had too much sun today," Iva's mother said, getting up. "Time we all went home. Iva, go tell the others we're leaving."

Back at the beach house, everyone got ready for bed. Iva waited outside the bathroom door. Heaven brushed her teeth so vigorously it sounded like she was scrubbing the side of a battleship.

When it was her turn, Iva pretended to brush her teeth and wash her face. She held one of her braids under her nose. It smelled wonderfully funky.

On their sleeping porch, Heaven was dressed in her ladies' nightgown. The stuffed cat she'd won was perched on Heaven's side of the chest between their beds. She plumped her pillow and folded her extra blanket in exact thirds. Then she knelt by her bed for her prayers.

"God bless Mama and Daddy and Howard and Hunter. God bless Aunt Sissy and Uncle Sonny and Arden and Lily Pearl. God bless Yard Sale and Miz Compton and Cazy Sparkle. Oh! And bless London Howdyshell, she's new on my list. . . ."

Iva climbed into bed, grumpy because Heaven had left Iva off her prayer list again. She shoved her feet down toward the bottom of the bed. For once she wished her sheets were nice and smooth, like Heaven's. Her toes touched something gritty. She got out again and flung the covers to the floor. Sand!

She brushed sand vigorously from her sheets. "How come you put sand in my bed?"

"I don't appreciate you accusing me, Iva."

"Who else would have done it?"

"Maybe it's from your own grubby feet!" Heaven moved her stuffed cat a half an inch to the right. Then she got into bed and turned the light out.

Neither of them said good night.

Iva twisted on her wrinkled sheets, trying to get comfortable. She had nearly dozed off when she heard an odd noise from behind the sleeping porch. A metallic flink, flink, flink.

"What is that?" Sleep was impossible, so she got up and flicked more sand from her bed.

Heaven raised herself on her elbow and looked toward the cottage behind them. All the lights blazed.

"It's coming from there," she said. "I think somebody's throwing silverware in a drawer."

"That's exactly what it is. Who does their dishes in the middle of the night?"

Flink, flink. Flink. Those old ladies next door were going to drive her crazy, one fork at a time. She got back into bed and pulled the pillow over her head.

By the SEA, by the SEA, by the beautiful SEA!

Iva sat up so fast her pillow sailed to the floor. "Don't tell me—"

"They're singing," Heaven groaned from the darkness.

"You and ME, you and ME, oh, how HAPPY we'll be!"

Iva couldn't stand it. If anybody could make the night peaceful, it was Heaven. With the power of that lucky penny, she could do anything.

"Heaven, do me a favor. Pray for them to shut up."

"I'm not a machine you put a token in and get a prayer," Heaven said, insulted.

"WHEN each wave comes a-rolling IN—"

"Please?" Iva begged. "It'll be good practice for when you become a Sunday-school teacher."

"No."

"I'll make your bed the whole rest of the time we're here!"

"You don't know how to make a bed right."

"WE will duck or SWIM—"

Iva played her last card, flattery. "Will you show me how to make a bed? You're so good at it. And then I'll make both our beds all week."

"All right." Heaven sighed. She got out of bed and assumed her praying position. "Dear Lord, please make those ladies over there shut their yaps and go to sleep."

Amazingly, the lights in the cottage blinked out. Then there was silence. "It worked!" Iva cried. "Yippee!"

"Of course it worked." Heaven turned over to face the wall. "Don't forget our deal, Iva. I'm gonna watch to make sure you do the beds right."

Iva pulled her sheet up to her chin. She had traded sleep for a nonvacation chore, making beds. Worse, she would be supervised by Heaven, Queen of Housekeeping.

She had nearly drifted off again when she heard another sound, above Heaven's puffing and snoring.

It was the front door, slowly opening and closing.

Someone was leaving the house. Iva sat up again. A car door chunked in the thick night air. Headlights flared across the porch, blinding Iva for a second.

It was Mr. Smith sneaking out, off on his

mysterious explorer-spy mission. Iva longed to follow him.

But she was so tired her eyes kept clunking shut. If Captain John Smith himself had come back and asked her to go exploring with him, she'd have had to tell him no.

"Iva!"

Iva cringed at the unmistakable smell of chocolate breath.

"Lily Pearl," she mumbled into her pillow. "Go back to bed."

Her sister slipped in beside her. "Iva."

"Wha . . . ?" Would this night ever end?

"I'm sorry about the Frisbee. It was a nice present."

"S'okay. Don' worry about it."

"You're my favorite sister of all." Lily Pearl slid quietly out of the bed and tiptoed out.

Iva stretched her legs and her toes touched something gritty. Sand.

Chapter Seven

Sugar and Salt

"You work on that side," Howard ordered Iva, pointing with his plastic shovel. He was coated with sand, like a catfish rolled in cornmeal.

"Aye, aye." Iva tossed a pailful of sand over her shoulder.

Each day Howard dug industriously from the second they hit the beach until it was time to go home. His hole was about three feet deep and almost as wide. Mike, the lifeguard, gave them orange cones to put around the edge so people wouldn't fall in.

Lily Pearl skittered crablike around the top of the pit. She patted the sand Iva and Howard threw out into a neat mound.

"I'm making a mountain," she said.

Iva scraped out another pailful. A shadow

darkened the sky. It was either a solar eclipse or Heaven's large self.

"What?" Iva looked up at her cousin.

"We're going in the water," Heaven asked. "Wanna come?" London was with her, a boogie board tucked under her arm.

Lily Pearl handed a small white pebble to London. "Is this a pearl?"

"That's just a dumb old rock," London replied curtly, tossing the pebble.

Lily Pearl drooped with disappointment.

London wasn't very good with little kids, Iva thought. Maybe because she was an only child.

"Lily Pearl, did you know pearls come from oysters?" Iva said, accidentally-on-purpose shoveling sand on London's feet.

"No. What's an oyster?"

"It's an animal that lives in a seashell. A grain of sand gets in their shell and the oyster turns it into a pearl so it won't be irritated."

"Too bad people can't do the same," Heaven said. "Iva, are you coming or not?"

Iva crawled out of the hole. She was itchy and hot. "Okay."

"We're gonna surf," London said as they walked down to the water. "When I lived in California, we went surfing all the time. I'm teaching Heaven."

Heaven wore a bathing-suit top and baggy knee-length nylon shorts she had bought at Cazy Sparkle's yard sale. The shorts were patterned with orange palm trees and lime-green coconuts.

"Those are boys' shorts," Iva told her.

"Nuh-uh. They are vintage surfing jams, I'll have you to know. Isn't it lucky I picked the Surfing card from my Daily Life at the Beach deck?"

"You and those stupid cards," Iva said. "Why don't you just grab a suitcase and put on whatever's in it? Live dangerously."

London stopped at the water's edge. "I can take one of you out at a time. Who wants to go first?"

"I know how to surf," Iva lied. "I'm gonna swim. At least fifty miles."

"Fifty miles!" London stared at her. "You'd be all the way in the ocean!"

"Okay, ten." Iva couldn't really swim well at all. She mainly dog-paddled.

"Watch out for jellyfish," London warned.

"What's a jellyfish?"

London pointed to a clear, round, blobby thing lying in the wet sand. "That. If you touch one or it touches you, it'll sting like crazy. My father says the tide brought them in today."

Iva had never seen anything so disgusting in her whole entire life. The jellyfish looked like a huge loogie somebody had hocked up.

"Ew, gross," said Heaven.

"It stings?" Iva remembered the stingray that had attacked Captain John Smith.

"You bet," London said. "I got stung once. It hurt a lot."

Iva looked dubiously at the bay. "But you're going in?"

"Sure. Once we're out a ways, there won't be hardly any." She splashed into the water, the boogie board balanced on her head. "Heaven, you coming?"

Iva knew Heaven was terrified of anything that stung. If she saw a little sweat bee, she'd thrash her arms like a windmill, run inside the house, and bolt the door.

Heaven kicked off her flip-flops. "Wait for me!"

"Aren't you scared?" Iva asked. For once, she was hoping Heaven would stick with her.

"Not me! I've got my lucky penny!" Then she hurtled into the waves.

Iva couldn't believe it. Her great big sissy of a cousin, who wouldn't make a move without drawing a Daily Life card, was swimming in jellyfish-infested waters!

"C'mon, Iva!" Heaven called. "It's okay. Really!"

It was put up or shut up. But all Iva could think about was Captain John Smith being zapped by that giant stingray. He had thought he was going to die. And he was an explorer, who braved starvation and wild animals!

Slowly Iva waded into the water. She whipped her head around. A big jellyfish bobbed at her right. Stringy things hung down from its slimy body. Stingers! Quickly she backed away. Then she spotted two baby jellyfish, each no bigger than a quarter. But they were still deadly. She swished around them.

Heaven and London were out where the waves were bigger. They lay on their stomachs across the boogie board, paddling and giggling.

Something brushed Iva's calf. She pictured hundreds of jellyfish and stingrays lurking just below the murky surface. She thrashed back to shore, leaving a wake the size of a tidal wave's. Unable to stop, she tore through the middle of a little kid's sand castle.

"Mama!" the boy bawled. "That girl wrecked my castle!"

"Sorry," Iva told him and kept running.

Why did she ever think a trip to the beach would be exciting? So far, she'd lost her mother's camera, been kept awake by fork-slinging old ladies, and was now being chased by poisonous sea creatures.

Iva collapsed at the dock to catch her breath. A double-decker boat was chugging alongside. People sat on benches on the top. On the main deck, more people clustered at the rail.

When the boat was tied up, tourists with wind-blown hair and sunburned faces filed off. Many wore cameras around their necks. Iva looked at the cameras longingly.

The sign on the ticket booth said that the *Chesapeake Zephyr* cruised "Captain John Smith's Bay" twice each day. Tickets cost ten dollars for a one-hour tour.

If she could ride on the *Chesapeake Zephyr*, she'd see the island where Captain John Smith had wanted to be buried. She might even see Chessie again! She could borrow somebody's camera and take Chessie's picture quick, before anyone else spotted her.

Then she'd sell the picture for a bunch of money and buy her mother a new camera.

Best of all, she'd be a world-famous discoverer of sea serpents. London Howdyshell would beg to be Iva's best friend. And maybe Iva would let her.

Arden posed wearing one old brown sandal and one new purple sandal. The toenails of her brown-sandaled foot were painted pink. The toenails of her other foot were red.

"Which looks the best?" she asked Iva. "Don't rush. Think about it."

Iva was trying to figure out how she'd get the extra five dollars for the boat ticket. But she pretended to ponder this vital question. "Red toenails."

"Really? I think so, too." Then Arden frowned. "What's wrong with the other foot?"

Iva's mother came into the living room. "No one leaves this house tonight until the sand is back outside where it belongs. Who left these wet towels on the sofa?"

"Iva!" Heaven replied at the same time that Iva said, "Heaven!"

Mrs. Honeycutt flashed her hard eyes and everyone got busy.

Hunter swept and Arden picked up beach toys, stray flip-flops, and bathing-suit bottoms. Heaven carried the wet towels outside to hang on the line in the backyard.

"If you see those old ladies, tell them to be quiet tonight," Iva said.

She gathered Lily Pearl's vast shell collection, shocked that there were any shells left on the beach. She wondered why the shells looked so pretty wet but were so drab and ordinary after they'd dried.

The dull shells reminded her of Heaven, who still clung to her souvenir money.

Maybe Iva could bargain with her. She was already making Heaven's bed. What else could she do for her cousin?

"Where are Howard and Lily Pearl?" Aunt Sissy Two asked. "I asked them an hour ago to brush their teeth."

"They're out back, playing bride and groom," said Hunter.

Hermy the hermit crab made scuttling sounds in his cage on the windowsill.

"The only one who listens around here is that crab," Aunt Sissy Two declared.

At last the house was straight, everyone was reasonably clean, and both of Arden's feet matched. Iva and Heaven each had three dollars to spend on snacks. They walked together to the boardwalk.

"I think I'll buy my souvenir tonight," Heaven said, going into Surfside Gifts. She picked up a box covered with whirly seashells.

Iva's heart skipped a beat. Now tightwad Heaven wanted to spend her money!

"You don't want that," she advised. "The glue looks cheap. I bet the shells drop off before you get it home."

Heaven set the box down and picked up a picture frame. Iva found something wrong with it, too. Getting her cousin's five bucks wasn't going to be easy.

"What about this?" Heaven held up a T-shirt with the words I HAD A BLAST AT STINGRAY POINT printed across the front.

"The words go under your armpits," Iva said. "You'll have to keep raising your arms so people can read it." She flapped her own arms like a chicken.

Heaven refolded the shirt. "I know what you're doing, Iva."

"What?"

"You're gonna tell me something ugly is perfect so I'll buy it. Then you'll go buy something really nice after I've wasted my money."

"I just don't want you to get ripped off is all," Iva said. Unless it's by me, she thought.

They went back outside. Arden and Hunter were talking to Mike.

"The Sno-Cone stand is right there," he told

Arden, who was standing almost inside it.

"Are you sure?" she asked. "I still don't see it. Maybe you could show us."

As he walked away, shaking his head, Arden exclaimed, "Spruce Up, phooey! He didn't even look at my feet. That stupid Love Teller lied!"

"I still have my fortune to try," Hunter said. "One of us still has a chance."

Iva was about to ask Heaven to lend her five dollars when London Howdyshell came over with her mother.

"You know the best way to eat boardwalk food?" asked London.

"Hey to you, too," Iva said. She didn't want London to see her trying to chisel money from Heaven. Maybe she could send London away for a few minutes.

"Sugar and salt," London replied. "First, you eat a bunch of sweet stuff. And then you eat salty stuff to get the sugar taste out of your mouth. Then you go back to sugar."

London's mother took a twenty-dollar bill

from her purse. "Honey, don't eat too much, or you'll get sick. Bring me back some change."

Iva goggled at the twenty. London must have been rich. If *she* dropped her mother's camera in the bay, she'd probably buy a new one in two minutes. A new plan formed in the back of Iva's mind.

"You gonna spend all that money on junk food?" she asked blandly. "You could get sick."

London fixed her dark eyes on her, taking the bait. "So what if I do?"

Iva knew that London was up for another challenge. "Bet you I get sicker!"

"Have you gone insane?" Heaven said. "Betting on getting sick? That's—sick."

"Five bucks?" Iva offered.

"Deal!" London swept them down the boardwalk toward the food stalls. "Bring on the sugar!"

They hit the cotton-candy stand first. Iva got the largest-size cotton candy, bigger even than Heaven's head. The breeze blew the spun sugar into Iva's face. Soon, most of her cotton candy webbed her hair and eyebrows.

London, walking backward out of the wind, ate hers down to the paper stick.

Next, London bought a big box of saltwater taffy for them to share. Iva grabbed a huge handful. She crammed taffy into her mouth as fast as Heaven unwrapped it.

When she had a dozen or so pieces in her mouth, she tried to chew, but her jaws wouldn't close.

"'Elp 'e," she said gummily.

Heaven held Iva's nose with one hand and pushed her chin up with the other. Pink drool oozed from Iva's lips. Heaven worked Iva's jaws up and down until she was able to swallow some of the taffy.

Meanwhile, London polished off the rest of

the box. Iva couldn't figure out how the other girl did it. Her face wasn't even sticky.

"Time to switch," London said. "We do it gradually. Sugar and salt."

They each bought the biggest-size bucket of kettle-cooked popcorn. Her teeth still glommed with taffy, Iva could barely eat half of her popcorn. Heaven took care of the rest of the bucket.

"Now we go straight to salt. Ever had fried mushrooms?" London asked.

Iva was slap broke, and junk food was expensive. She gazed woozily at the store's sign, advertising small, medium, and large plates of fried mushrooms. "Aren't you feeling sick yet?"

"Not a bit." London placed two large orders.

Iva took Heaven aside. "Lend me your food money."

"Iva, you have to quit. This is crazy, even for you."

"Forget it!" Iva caught sight of Lily Pearl lollygagging behind her mother and Aunt Sissy Two.

Her little sister gripped her plastic purse. Iva flew across the boardwalk.

"Lily Pearl," she said sweetly. "Can I borrow your five dollars?"

"No." Then Lily Pearl said, "What for?"

"It's a secret. Something *reeaal* nice." Iva smiled. "Maybe for you."

Lily Pearl took a much-folded five-dollar bill from her purse. "Are you getting me the bride necklace at the snooveneer store?"

"It'll be a surprise! Don't tell Mama. Thanks!" Iva snatched the money and paid for a plate of fried mushrooms, which she could barely choke down. London's plate was already clean except for a swipe of grease.

"Back to sugar," London announced. "Fried cheesecake bites. Mmm!"

Iva handed over the rest of Lily Pearl's money and received a green basket with six deep-fat-fried cheesecake bites resting uneasily on a square of grease-soaked paper.

London took her basket to the other side of

the boardwalk, near a trash can. Iva turned her back. She could barely stuff down her own food, much less watch London.

The cheesecake bites tasted as awful as they looked. Iva's stomach began to rumble. One more cheesecake bite to go. Gamely she gobbled it whole.

Her stomach lurched. Iva dropped the basket.

Heaven ran over. "I think London's cheating! You can stop this right now!"

It was too late. Clutching her middle, Iva staggered over to the trash can. As she leaned over, a pile of fried mushrooms stared back at her.

Iva pulled away from the revolting sight and threw up magnificently on the steps.

"Ewww!" Heaven pinched her nostrils shut. "Right where people walk. Gross!"

Iva wouldn't have cared if she had thrown up in the White House. London had cheated!

London came over, took one look at Iva's mess, and gagged. Pink-tinged vomit gushed clear across the boardwalk. People leaped out of the way.

"Wow!" Heaven said. "London puked way more than you did, Iva."

It wasn't possible. Iva had eaten more! But London had managed to throw up more, somehow. Iva had lost the bet and now owed London five dollars.

Plus, she had broken rule number three. She'd taken Lily Pearl's souvenir money for nothing.

Chapter Eight

The Tattle-Teller

Flink. Flink. Flink.

Iva plunked each knife in the drawer as she dried it. The old ladies in the cottage had tossed silverware and sung half the night again. Since they were probably sleeping in, Iva figured she'd give them a wake-up call.

Cheerios crunched under her bare feet. Broken crayons lay scattered on the table. The little kids made such a mess.

After breakfast, Lily Pearl had cornered Iva wanting to know where her bride necklace was. Iva told her to wait for the surprise. She hated fibbing to her little sister, but what else could she do?

Arden and Hunter slouched into the kitchen and sat at the table.

"I heard," Arden said as she began painting

her fingernails red and pink, "that the board-walk starts jumping around ten. We always come home too early."

"So, we should stay out later?" Hunter asked.

Flink.

"It's the only way to meet boys; maybe see Mike—"

Flink. Flink.

"Iva, must you make that annoying noise?" Arden complained.

"Yes," Iva said. "Mama will never let you stay out in a million years."

"She won't know, if a certain blabbermouth keeps quiet. Or I'll tell her you haven't taken a bath since we got here."

Iva sniffed under her arm. "How'd you know? Do I stink?" She hoped so.

"Like a wet dog behind a hot woodstove," said Hunter.

Iva picked up a slotted spoon from the dish drainer. It was too big for the silverware drawer. She opened another drawer, which contained large utensils. As she dropped the spoon in, she spied something in the corner and pulled it out: a metal ring loaded with keys of all shapes and sizes.

She'd have bet her *National Geographic* collection that one of those keys fit the lock on the door in the living room. The door that led upstairs to Mr. Smith's forbidden rooms.

"So, how're we gonna stay out later?" Hunter asked Arden.

"Leave it to me." Arden glanced at Iva and clammed up.

But Iva had her ears trained on the front door. Did she hear it open and close? From the bloodcurdling yells in the bathroom, she knew her mother and Aunt Sissy Two were getting the little kids ready. Heaven was still putting on her costume for the day.

That left Mr. Smith. He must have just gone out.

"Everybody ready to hit the beach?" Iva's mother came in. She checked her straw bag.

"Hmm. Still can't find my camera."

"I am!" Howard yelled. "I'm gonna dig in my hole all day and all night!"

Iva slowly wiped the counters. "Mama, I'll finish cleaning up the kitchen and come down in a few minutes, okay?"

Her mother put her hand on Iva's forehead. "You feeling all right, Iva-kins?"

Actually, Iva's stomach hadn't recovered from last night's junk-food binge. She had barely touched her breakfast. And she felt a little sicker hearing that her mother had just missed her camera.

"I got a little—um, back-door trouble," she fibbed.

"If you have the runs, you shouldn't go out in the sun," Aunt Sissy Two advised.

"I'll stay home with you," her mother said.

"No!" Iva realized she had gone too far. "I mean, I'm okay. I'll just sweep the floor and pick up these crayons. I'm right behind you."

Heaven came in, dressed in her "Sun Tan"

outfit, a yellow two-piece bathing suit that revealed a billboard-size expanse of stomach. When she saw Iva with the broom, she threw her cousin a suspicious look, then walked outside with the others.

Iva raced into the living room with the key ring. With shaking hands, she tried the first key. Didn't fit. Neither did the second. The very last key turned in the lock.

She opened the door. A steep flight of stairs led straight up to the second floor.

She crept up the steps. At the top, two rooms branched off from a short hallway.

Iva went into the sitting room. The desk was covered with papers, and there was a book, *The Atlas of Amphibians and Reptiles in Virginia*. Then she noticed a stack of printed forms weighted by a metal cup of sharpened pencils.

She peeked at the form on top. Someone had printed neatly, *quiet moving creek channeling through a swamp with aquatic vegetation*. Weird.

A map of Stingray Point was spread out on a

coffee table. The map showed marshes, creeks, and wooded areas. Several places on the map were circled in red and connected by red lines.

Iva traced the lines with her finger. Was this Mr. Smith's secret-discovery-spy route? What did he do at those red-circled places? Was he looking for something? Pirates' gold? If so, how did his notes on swamps and water plants fit in?

A CD player anchored a corner of the map. Stuck to one side was a label that read, DO NOT USE TO CALL. Of course Iva was eaten up with curiosity. She punched the ON button.

The sound of static was followed by dripping noises, like raindrops hitting leaves. Then: *WAAAAAAAAAHHHHHHHH!*

The inhuman cry almost knocked Iva flat. What was that horrible sound? It must be Chessie! Only a sea serpent could make such a loud, unearthly call.

Mr. Smith was trying to find Chessie! It made perfect sense. The sea serpent probably had a nest or something in the swamps.

Iva looked for more signs of sea-monster hunting. On a shelf in the bookcase she spotted a compass, thermometer, kitchen timer, flashlight, some extra batteries . . . and a camera.

The camera was almost exactly like her mother's. She picked it up. If she had had Heaven's luck, Mr. Smith would simply have given her the camera. But she didn't have a lucky penny. She'd have to make her own luck.

Maybe she'd help him find Chessie's nest. She knew the sea serpent's call now. She could go with Mr. Smith on his secret route. He was probably old, and old people got tired (except those ladies in the cottage). After they found Chessie's nest, Mr. Smith would be so grateful he'd offer a reward.

Iva played out the scene in her head.

"Please, take whatever you want," Mr. Smith would say. "No," she'd tell him, "I only helped for the experience." "I insist," he'd say. Reluctantly she would pick out the camera. "To remember you by," she'd say modestly.

Her daydream was interrupted by the sound of someone coming up the steps. She hadn't heard the front door, but it must be Mr. Smith! Spies were experts at sneaking.

Iva looked desperately around, but there was no way out. She was considering sliding behind the drapes when Heaven puffed into the room.

"I thought you went to the beach," Iva said, still shaken by the sound of Chessie's call.

"I came back for my lucky penny," Heaven said. "I forgot it. Then I saw this door open. What're you doing up here?"

Iva didn't for a second believe Heaven's flimsy excuse. She knew her cousin had doubled back just to catch her. "Mr. Smith left the door open. I only—"

"You broke the rule, Iva Honeycutt," Heaven stated. "You broke all the rules."

"What're you, the official rule keeper?"

Heaven ticked off Iva's crimes on her fingertips. "First, you got in the water without permission. Then you didn't watch Lily Pearl. Last night you took that poor little kid's money. And now you're in this man's room."

Iva wondered if she'd find Heaven in Mr. Smith's book, under "Reptiles." "How come you haven't tattled to my mother?" she asked. "Saving it up to tell her all at once?"

That was it. Heaven was planning to clobber Iva with one great big tattle tale.

Heaven was like the Love Teller machine in

the arcade. Put a token in the Tattle-Teller and the answer light landed on everything Iva had ever done wrong.

Heaven stared at the camera in Iva's hands. "Were you gonna steal that camera?"

"No!" Iva put the camera down on the table. "I was just looking at it."

"Something funny is going on." Heaven made one eye squinty. "Yesterday, Aunt Sissy couldn't find her camera. This morning, she said she still couldn't find it."

"So?" A goose walked over Iva's grave. Heaven knew.

"You took it, didn't you? I bet you broke it." Heaven sashayed out of the room in her yellow two-piece bathing suit, singing, *"I have a se-cret!"*

Iva ran after her. "You don't know anything, Heaven Honeycutt! Tell all you want! I don't care one teeny little speck!"

But Iva did care. She was in huge trouble. As soon as Heaven was out the front door, she hurried down the steps, locked the door to the stairs, and tossed the key ring back in the kitchen drawer. Then she sprinted outside and down the street to the beach.

Red and yellow umbrellas sprouted from the sand like colorful toadstools. People sprawled on blankets. Radios played. Little kids shrieked in the waves. Everyone was having a great time.

Everyone but Iva. Life as she knew it was about to end.

At the boat dock, passengers climbed aboard the *Chesapeake Zephyr* for the morning tour. Iva wished more than anything that she had been with them. She'd have paid the boat driver extra to let her off on the Maryland side of the bay.

She spotted her mother's and aunt's matching beach chairs. Arden and Hunter lay on towels near Mike's lifeguard stand. Lily Pearl and Howard were digging in a hole. Heaven was nowhere in sight.

Maybe she'd fallen in the hole. No. Not with that lucky penny. If only Iva had a lucky coin, too.

How would she make one get flat? She could put a penny under Heaven's chair, but that would take too long. She needed help right now.

Iva thought fast. Suppose she started talking to her mother and kept on talking and talking and talking? When Heaven showed up to tattle, she wouldn't be able to get a word in sideways.

She jogged through the sand to her mother's chair. "Hi, Mama!"

"Feeling better?" her mother asked, giving her a squeeze.

"Yeah. It was just one of those—half-hour bugs."

"What?"

Iva sat in the sand beside her mother. "You know, like a twenty-four-hour bug? Only this one was shorter."

"Iva, you take the cake," her mother said, laughing.

I also took your camera, Iva thought, and lost it. "Mama, see that boat out there? It goes around the Chesapeake Bay," she said expansively, "where Captain John Smith went. I think we should ride on it."

"How much are the tickets?"

"Only ten dollars. That's pretty cheap, considering all the education we'd get."

Iva was laying it on thick.

"Only ten dollars? Iva, there are eight of us. Do you realize how much it will cost for all of us to go?"

Iva tried to do the math in her head, but couldn't remember if she was supposed to drop or carry the one. "How much?"

"Eighty bucks."

"How about if just you and me went?" Iva glanced around.

Where was Heaven? Lowering the boom on Iva was Heaven's favorite occupation. It wasn't like her to miss an opportunity this good.

Her mother shook her head. "Would that be fair to the others?"

"How about just me?"

"Don't be ridiculous. You can't go by yourself."

"Sure I can! Just give me an advance on my allowance. I'll pay you back when we get home." If she could keep talking about the boat and convince her mother to let her go, she'd kill two birds with one stone.

"No."

Out of the corner of her eye, Iva glimpsed a two-piece yellow bathing suit. She shifted position so she was blocking her mother's view.

"Mama, have you seen the hole Howard dug? Isn't it something? I wouldn't be surprised if he didn't get in the paper. I bet it's the deepest hole any kid ever dug on this beach. Or any beach anywhere in the world. And Howard is only five years old! I bet he becomes a professional hole-digger when he grows up."

Aunt Sissy Two looked at her over her sunglasses. "Iva, you sure you're okay?"

"Never felt better," Iva rattled on. "That's because I had a glass of orange juice for breakfast. They say that orange juice is liquid sunshine. Sunshine in a glass! Do you believe that? I do!"

The two-piece yellow bathing suit walked by. It wasn't Heaven after all.

Iva stood up and scanned the beach. Heaven had to be there somewhere. Her eyes lit on Hunter, who was performing a perfect cartwheel in front of the lifeguard stand.

"Look, Hunter is doing tricks!" Iva said. She saw Arden scowl at Hunter. Iva knew Arden couldn't turn a cartwheel if her life depended on it.

Then Iva's older sister got up off her towel, tugged her bathing-suit bottom over her butt, and took two tottering steps. The back of her hand went to her forehead as if she were dizzy.

She staggered to the lifeguard stand and sagged like a sack of flour. Then, with a little moan and an exaggerated eye-roll, Arden swooned.

Iva noticed that Arden didn't crash face-first in the sand, but fell prettily, with one arm flung over her face and her toes pointed like a ballet dancer's.

Iva's mother jumped up. "Oh, my stars and stripes! Arden's fainted!"

Aunt Sissy Two scrambled out of her chair. Mike leaped off the lifeguard stand and bent over Arden's motionless body.

Just then, Heaven and London came running up. They were wet from swimming.

"Mama!" Heaven exclaimed. "Guess what? London's mother and father asked me to go with them on a boat trip tomorrow! Is it okay? Can I go?"

Iva's knees buckled. She toppled over in a heap.

Chapter Nine

Heaven's Secret

Nobody paid any attention to Iva. She got up and stumbled over to the lifeguard stand, where strangers had formed a crowd.

"Get back, please," Mike ordered, opening his first-aid kit. "Give her some air."

Arden lay on her back. Her eyelids flickered just a little.

She's faking! Iva thought.

"My poor baby! Should we call an ambulance?" Mrs. Honeycutt asked Mike.

"Let me try smelling salts." He rummaged through his first-aid kit and took out a white capsule. Crushing it between his fingers, he held it under Arden's nose. The strong smell of ammonia mingled with Arden's suntan oil.

Arden's eyelashes fluttered. "Where am I?"

she asked weakly. "I can't move."

Iva could not believe the act her sister was putting on. She reached over and pinched the back of Arden's knee.

"Ow! You little—" Arden sat bolt upright and slapped Iva's arm.

"I thought you couldn't move!" Hunter said accusingly. "You big fat phony, Arden Honeycutt! You stole my 'Act Desperate' before I could use it!"

"The way you were showing off, Miss Circus Acrobat, I had to do something."

"Should I call the EMT guys?" Mike asked. He looked confused.

Mrs. Honeycutt helped Arden to her feet. "She's fine. Thank you for your help, young man." She led Arden away as the crowd broke up.

Iva hopped along beside them. Her mother was white-hot mad. It was nice that somebody else was in trouble for a change.

"What you did was very foolish," Iva's mother told Arden. "What if someone needed the lifeguard for a real emergency? Don't you ever pull a stunt like that again!"

"Get your towel," Aunt Sissy Two ordered Hunter. "Arden's, too. Bring your things over by us where we can keep an eye on you two."

"See what you did?" Hunter said, glaring at Arden.

Arden and Hunter spread their towels next to their mothers' chairs. They lay down and simmered, not talking to anyone, not even each other.

Heaven was still waiting for an answer. "Mama, you didn't say if I could go on the boat trip with London tomorrow. Can I?"

"We'll pay, of course," London put in, like she could persuade anybody's parents.

"A free trip, Mama! Can I go?"

"Not now, Heaven," said Aunt Sissy Two.

Even Heaven knew enough to drop the subject. "Let's go back in the water," she said to London. They took off, giggling and holding hands like best friends.

Iva watched them. Heaven was going on the boat trip. Could life possibly get any more unfair?

"Iva, don't look so glum," her mother said. "Tell you what. We'll make pizza tonight instead of going out."

"We have to stay in?" Iva said, wondering how this was supposed to cheer her up.

"We don't want any dumb old homemade pizza," Arden said sullenly, forgetting she was still in the doghouse.

"Yeah, we want to go on the boardwalk," added Hunter.

Aunt Sissy Two frowned. "Count yourself lucky we didn't send you both back to the house for the rest of the day."

Arden shot Hunter a look. Hunter gave a slight nod. Iva caught the exchange and suspected they were up to something.

But she had her own worries. If they stayed home all evening, Heaven would have plenty of time to spring her tattle-trap.

* * *

Supper was torture. Iva could only nibble at her pizza, waiting for Heaven to deliver her knockout punch.

But Heaven rattled on about her trip instead. "London says the boat carries eighty-nine passengers, but only thirty can sit on top. London says we'll get seats on top, no problem."

Iva was itching to ask Heaven if she was going to keep quoting London for the rest of her life, but didn't want to call attention to herself. Heaven had a boatload of tattling stored up, yet she didn't even glance in Iva's direction.

"We'll hear all about your trip when you get back tomorrow," Aunt Sissy Two told Heaven. "Let someone else talk."

"Just one more thing." Heaven turned to Iva's mother. "Aunt Sissy!"

Iva jumped like she'd been shot. This was it! Heaven was going to drop the bomb. In her final hour, Iva didn't even have a whole slice of pizza.

"Heaven, I'm right here," Iva's mother said. "What is it?"

"Will you French-braid my hair tomorrow? You do it best. I want my hair perfect for the boat trip."

"Of course," said Iva's mother. "Who wants more pizza?"

No one answered. Arden and Hunter sulked over their plates throughout the meal. Lily Pearl and Howard leaned on their elbows, half-asleep.

"I think everybody's played out," said Aunt Sissy Two. "Good thing we stayed in this evening. Heaven, will you and Iva clear the table? We need to get the little ones in the bathtub."

Arden, who'd been slumped in her seat like a marionette with cut strings, sprang to life and grabbed her aunt's plate. "We'll do the dishes, won't we, Hunter?"

"After that, we're going in our room," Hunter said, too loudly.

"Yeah, we have some letters to write, and then we'll go to sleep early." Arden slathered it on pretty thick, Iva noticed. Something was up.

Usually her sister had to be forced to bed with a cattle prod.

"I wish I had a picture of this," Iva's mother remarked to Aunt Sissy Two. "Our oldest girls actually volunteering to do the dishes!"

"Did you ever find your camera?" Aunt Sissy Two asked.

Mrs. Honeycutt shook her head. "I put it in my beach bag; haven't seen it since."

From across the table, Heaven aimed a beady-eyed look right at Iva and opened her mouth. Iva took a huge gulp of iced tea and choked, spraying tea all over herself.

Heaven's big moment for tattling passed as Iva's mother clapped Iva on the back, Arden and Hunter efficiently whisked plates away, and the little kids were herded, bleating like lambs, to the bathroom.

Iva went out onto the front porch and sat down on the steps to do some serious thinking. She couldn't live in fear of Heaven. She had to do something now.

Her idea of going with Mr. Smith on his secret route was a good one. But Mr. Smith's car wasn't parked in its usual spot, which meant he was out, possibly already on his nightly mission.

In her mind's eye she could see the map on the coffee table in Mr. Smith's room. The marshes began at the edge of town. The first red circle was only a few blocks from their house. All Iva had to do was wander around in the marsh until she heard Chessie make the terrible cry she'd heard on Mr. Smith's CD player. That would lead her right to the sea serpent's nest.

Nobody would miss her for a while. Arden and Hunter were slamming and banging in the kitchen. Her mother and Aunt Sissy Two were busy giving the little kids baths. Heaven was probably laying out her dumb old boat-trip outfit for tomorrow.

Iva stood up. She should change into her discovery shorts and get her flashlight. But Heaven would ask a million questions about where Iva was going. Captain John Smith hadn't always had his exploring equipment. She would do without, too!

She skipped down the porch steps, dodged around the corner of the house, and cut through the old ladies' yard. As she zigzagged down the next two streets to throw any trackers off her trail, she passed grown-ups walking dogs and kids on skateboards.

The last street dead-ended at the marsh. Tall trees and zillions of green plants seemed to swallow the world. Blackbirds shrieked in the tree-tops, and dragonflies zipped over the dark, grassy water.

Iva closed her eyes to summon all her discovering strength. Ahead lay uncharted wilderness that hid alligators and poisonous snakes and gigantic spiders . . . and one sea serpent.

When she opened her eyes, she saw two things that filled her with annoyance.

One was a paved bike path winding through the uncharted wilderness. A bike path! What, no signs that said, THIS WAY TO CHESSIE'S NEST?

The other annoying thing waved its lady-size hand in front of Iva's face.

"Are you in a trance?" Heaven asked, snapping her fingers.

"What are you doing here?" Iva could not believe it. All of her zigging and zagging had been useless.

"I watched you leave. You didn't tell anybody. I followed you to bring you back so you won't get in trouble." Heaven stared at her. "Your face is all red. Are you feeling okay?"

Iva was surprised her head didn't explode from anger. "I'm fine! I came out here by myself for a reason."

"What reason?"

"None of your beeswax." She knew Heaven wouldn't budge until Iva confessed her mission. Or told a whale of a lie. She decided a lie was safer.

"If you must know, I'm really upset that London's taking you on the boat trip and not me. So I just had to be alone." She hung her head.

Acting wounded was even better than fighting. Dragging her feet like a worn-out buffalo, Iva shuffled down the path into the marsh.

Heaven hurried to catch up. "Maybe London will take you on the boat next."

"Yeah, right. How many times are London's parents going to ride that boat?" Iva picked up her pace, hoping to lose her naturally slower cousin.

Heaven chugged along beside Iva like she was riding a motorcycle. "Iva, you know why London likes me? Because I don't plan every minute of my day like you do. I'm free as a bird, like she is."

A bolt of lightning should have struck Heaven just then, Iva thought. "What about your Daily Life at the Beach cards?" she said. "Does free-as-a-bird London know about them?"

The path narrowed, and they could no longer walk side by side. Thick vines with leaves like elephant ears brushed Iva's knees.

"You're just jealous," Heaven snorted, slapping at a fan-shaped leaf. "London and I have a lot more in common—"

Just then, a sound ripped through the marsh. *WAAAAAAAAAAHHH!*

Fine hairs rose along Iva's arms. That was the exact same cry that was on Mr. Smith's CD player! She'd have known it anywhere! Only the sea monster could make that inhuman call.

"Did you hear that?" Iva whispered.

"What—?" Heaven began, but Iva yanked her down so that they were crouching in the middle of the path.

WAAAAHHHH!

They must be very close to the nest, Iva figured, her heart thumping. She hadn't figured on making the discovery with Heaven tagging along. But maybe it was a good thing. Since Iva didn't have a camera to take a picture of Chessie on her nest, Heaven would be a witness.

"Listen," Iva said, lowering her voice. "Whatever happens, don't be scared. I don't think she'll bother us. She knows me, sort of."

"Scared of what? Who knows you?" Heaven shook off Iva's grip and stood up.

WAAAHHHH!

The cry was almost upon them. Somehow the serpent was moving swiftly through the shallow waters of the marsh. Chessie must have had legs! And the monster sounded very hungry.

Iva stood up and stuck out her chin bravely. If this was truly the end, she would not go down like a coward.

Around the bend of the bike path came a young couple pushing a pink stroller. The baby girl inside the stroller was bawling her lungs out.

"Sorry," the mother said as they swerved around Iva and Heaven with the stroller. "She needs her nap."

"*Waaaaaaaahhhhh!*" The baby's cry grew fainter as the young couple hustled up the path.

Iva stared after them. A baby. How could she have made such a mistake? Was she losing her touch as a great discoverer?

"What was all that about?" Heaven asked. "That stuff about being scared and somebody bothering us?"

"Nothing. Just forget it."

Heaven pointed her finger at her temple and rotated it in the classic gesture that meant "You're cuckoo." "I think you were out in the sun too long today. Your brain is fried."

By some miracle, nobody had missed either of them. Arden's and Hunter's bedroom door was closed tight. Iva's mother was trying to dry off a seal-slick Lily Pearl. Howard was zonked out on his sofa bed in the living room.

Trying to avoid attention, Iva went into the bathroom and wet her toothbrush as usual. She ran her tongue over her teeth. They felt delightfully coated. Her back teeth were packed with popcorn hulls. Her braids smelled funky. She loved being filthy.

But tonight had been a complete failure. Iva couldn't catch a break. Only Heaven had a lucky penny. Only Heaven was going to ride the

Chesapeake Zephyr with London tomorrow. Only Heaven was going to drip pure luck the rest of her life. And Iva was going to bust rocks the rest of her life, for losing her mother's camera.

On the sleeping porch, Heaven was kneeling by her bed. Her head was bent and her lips were moving.

"Aren't you done praying yet?" Iva asked. Then she heard the rustle of paper.

Heaven wasn't saying her nightly prayers. She was counting money.

Iva jumped on Heaven's bed in a flash. "Where'd you get all that?"

"It's mine!" Heaven stacked the bills. "I brought it from home."

"You've been holding out! How much you got?"

"Twenty-seven dollars. I'm gonna use some of it to buy presents for Daddy and Miz Compton. And . . . something for London."

"London!"

"She's my friend. She's nice to me." Heaven's tone implied Iva wasn't.

With that much money, Iva could have bought her mother a new camera. Maybe even paid the money she owed London and paid back Lily Pearl, too.

She licked her lips. This had to be handled delicately. "I don't suppose you'd let me borrow it. For a really good cause."

"What cause?" Heaven flipped through the bundle of cash. "You mean your mother's camera that you lost?"

"Please; it's a matter of life and death." Iva cast her eyes down, trying to look humble and long-suffering.

"I might loan it to you," Heaven said slowly. "For thirty percent interest."

"Thirty percent! That's . . ." Iva didn't know how to do fractions.

"Eight dollars and ten cents," Heaven said. "Up front. Take it or leave it."

"If I had eight dollars and ten cents—" She stopped. "What's that noise?"

She heard a squeaking sound, like a window

being raised. Then something crashed into the snowball bushes; this was followed by a second crash.

Iva and Heaven ran over to the screen and peered into the darkness. Two shapes skulked across the backyard, whispering and giggling.

"Burglars!" Heaven cried. "Call the police!"

Iva had a suspicion. She fetched her flashlight and pointed it at the figures. Then she clicked it on. Two pale faces were trapped, wide-eyed, in the beam.

"It's Arden and Hunter," Iva said, "sneaking out to the boardwalk."

Chapter Ten

Lily Pearl's Revenge

Hunter screamed. Arden yelled, "Be quiet!"

Lights snapped on in the house. Iva's mother came out onto the sleeping porch.

"What's going on?" she asked.

"Look at the prowlers we caught," Iva said, dancing the flashlight beam around her sister's face.

"Turn that thing off!" Arden barked.

Iva's mother strode over to the screen door. "Arden and Hunter Honeycutt! Get your tiny heinies in the house right this minute."

"What's gonna happen to them, Aunt Sissy?" Heaven asked eagerly. She loved it when other people were in trouble.

"You and Iva go to bed. It's late." Iva's mother shut their door on her way out.

Iva climbed into her bed. "Boy, Arden really showed herself today. I bet she's grounded till she's seventy-five."

"Hunter, too," Heaven said from the darkness.

"I'm never gonna act like that over boys."

"Me, neither."

A companionable silence stretched between them. As always, Heaven fell asleep first, snoring like thunder.

The next morning, Iva launched herself out of bed. "Get up!"

"What's the rush?" Heaven said. "Oh! Hunter and Arden!"

They hurried to the kitchen, hoping to witness the downfall of their older sisters.

Arden and Hunter sat at the table, glowering at untouched plates of toast and eggs.

Across from them, Iva's mother and Aunt Sissy Two sipped coffee. Lily Pearl and Howard spooned dry Cheerios straight from the box, swinging their legs.

"The big girls are in trouble," Lily Pearl

cheerfully told Iva and Heaven.

"They got yelled at," Howard said.

"We're too late," Iva said to Heaven.

Aunt Sissy Two poured herself the last of the coffee. "Bread's in the toaster, girls. I'll fix your eggs."

"Thanks, Aunt Sissy," said Iva, sitting down. "I'm not that hungry."

"Scrambled for me," Heaven said. No excitement ever caused her to miss a meal.

Arden glared at Iva. "Thanks for the spotlight last night, warden."

"Don't blame me for your jailbreak." Iva snagged a stray Cheerio and ate it.

"Arden and Hunter have to stay within our sight the rest of the vacation," said Mrs. Honeycutt. "We've had enough of their shenanigans."

Iva wondered when Arden was going to try to shift her mother's hairy eyeballs off her and Hunter onto somebody else. She didn't have to wait long.

"Did you know Iva hasn't had a single shower since we came here?" Arden declared. "Over four days without a bath!"

Everyone stared at Iva. She shrank in her seat but imagined fumes radiating from her unwashed self. She could hide, but she still smelled bad.

"I wondered what that odor was," said her mother. She pulled one of Iva's braids toward her and sniffed it. "Your hair has mildewed!"

"That's not all Iva's done," Heaven said, forking eggs into her mouth at a terrific speed.

Iva gawked at her. Heaven was going to tattle now? At breakfast? When they were actually almost sort of getting along?

Heaven spoke casually. "She went out last night, too."

Mrs. Honeycutt turned to Iva. "Is this true?"

"Ask Heaven. She knows everything."

"I'm asking you."

"I just went out for a little walk." Iva pursed her lips at Arden. "Heaven came, too."

"I went after you." Heaven dabbed grape

147

jelly onto her second piece of toast.

"Nobody leaves this house without telling either me or Aunt Sissy Two," said Iva's mother. "Is that clear? Or do you all want to go home a day early?"

"We just want to stay later on the boardwalk," Arden said. "Can't we?"

"No." Mrs. Honeycutt's tone made it final.

Lily Pearl sucked in a gulp of air. "My money! Mama, Iva took my snooveneer five dollars! She said she was gonna buy me the pearl bride necklace! She promised!"

Iva began to sweat. What was this? National Take-a-Potshot-at-Iva Day?

"You took your sister's money? And promised to buy her a necklace?" her mother asked sternly.

"Where is it?" Lily Pearl demanded. "Where's my surprise?"

"It's been—delayed," Iva replied in desperation.

"Iva, give Lily Pearl her money back," her mother said. "And you and I will have a little talk later."

Heaven calmly reached for her third piece of toast. Why hadn't her cousin told the world that Iva had spent Lily Pearl's money on fried mushrooms and cheesecake bites?

Lily Pearl pointed her spoon at Iva. "You're fired as my favorite sister."

"It's our last day here," said Aunt Sissy Two. "Let's get ready for the beach."

At the beach, only Howard and Heaven seemed thrilled to be there. Howard leaped happily into his hole and began digging. Heaven met London and went swimming.

But Arden and Hunter grumped up like bullfrogs on their towels. Lily Pearl hung on the back of her mother's chair and whined about the bride necklace Iva had promised her.

Iva buried her feet in the sand and fretted. If only her mother would pronounce her sentence and get it over with.

Heaven and London came back, laughing and dripping water all over Iva.

"Do you mind?" Iva said crossly.

"At least you're getting a little clean," Heaven said, adding, as she turned to London, "Iva hasn't had a single shower since we came."

"I wondered what that smell was," London remarked.

"It's your upper lip." Iva snatched the towel Heaven was drying herself with. "That's mine."

"Excu-use me!"

"No excuse for you." In her rotten mood, Iva forgot that Heaven was one blab away from ruining Iva's entire life.

At last her mother and Aunt Sissy Two packed up their things. "Time for lunch," Iva's mother said. "Let's go, kids."

"See you at the boat dock at one thirty," London said to Heaven.

"I'll be there with bells on!"

Iva lifted her feet and shook sand all over Heaven. "Yeah, dumbbells."

"C'mon, Howard." Lily Pearl scrambled out of the hole.

His voice floated upward. "Go on without me!"

Aunt Sissy Two marched over to the pit. "Howard, don't keep us waiting."

"No! I'm not finished!"

Lily Pearl put her hands on her hips. "You get on out of that dumb old hole, Samuel Howard Honeycutt."

Iva joined Lily Pearl at the edge and looked down. Howard squatted toadlike at the bottom of the hole, looking fiercely up at them.

"Go on, Lily Pearl," Howard said. "I have work to do."

"Howard," said Aunt Sissy Two in that tone nobody argued with more than once.

He started to cry. "Let me dig! It's important!" He threw down his shovel. "Okay!"

As they all trooped back to the house, Iva

151

could hear Howard's snuffles. Lily Pearl walked a little ahead of him. For the first time since they were babies in diapers, Howard wanted to do something that Lily Pearl didn't.

Iva's mother fixed grilled-cheese sandwiches while Aunt Sissy Two poured sweet tea and set out a jar of dill-pickle chips and a dish of carrot sticks.

Iva picked at her sandwich and nibbled on half a carrot stick. The little kids filled a plate with nothing but pickle chips and went into the living room to eat on "Howard's bed," the sofa.

Heaven vacuumed up two sandwiches and five carrot sticks, then went out onto the sleeping porch and closed the door. She came out a few minutes later wearing a red-and-white-striped T-shirt, white shorts, and her canoe-size tennis shoes. She carried a navy blue windbreaker.

"Don't you look nautical," said Aunt Sissy Two.

Heaven grinned. "Today is our last day, and my last Daily Life at the Beach card is 'Sailboat Trip'! Isn't it cool the way that it worked out?"

"Only because you rigged the deck," Iva said. "And the *Chesapeake Zephyr* isn't a sailboat. You need a whole different outfit."

"You're just jealous London picked me instead of you."

Iva was jealous. And furious. Everything in Heaven's world was rosy, while Iva felt stuck in a hole deeper than Howard's.

"We have to talk about what we're doing tonight," Iva's mother said. "It's our last night. What should we do?"

"Well, me and Hunter could pick up dirt on the rug with tweezers," Arden suggested in her new, put-upon tone. "While you-all go out and have fun."

"Arden, you're becoming tiresome," said Mrs. Honeycutt. "Any other ideas?"

Heaven raised her hand.

"You're not in school, Heaven," Iva said.

"When I come back from my boat trip, I could tell stories about what I saw. Maybe we could have refreshments, like popcorn and lemonade—"

"I won't have time," Iva broke in.

Heaven looked at her. "What're you gonna be doing?"

"Math problems," Iva said. "I brought some with me in case, you know, I got bored."

"Iva . . ." her mother warned.

Aunt Sissy Two said, "Why don't we go out to dinner? We only have enough food for breakfast tomorrow."

"Sounds good," said Iva's mother. "The Crab Shack?"

"I hear the crab cakes are excellent," Heaven said.

Iva smirked. "You wouldn't know a crab cake if it bit you."

"Is that the place across from the beach photographer? Friend of you-know-who?" Arden asked, perking up.

"It is," Hunter said. "We can sit outside and eat and watch for—I mean, watch the people on the boardwalk."

"That's settled, then," said Aunt Sissy Two.

"The Crab Shack for supper. Now, let's spend our last afternoon on the beach. Peacefully."

"We'll come back early to get ready." Iva's mother tugged one of Iva's braids. "And you, missy, will take a long shower and wash that crusty head. It's full of sand."

"If there's any hot water left," Iva said. "Arden and Hunter take fifty showers a day, you know." Of course she'd have to take a shower. Wasn't this her lucky day?

Howard came into the kitchen with the empty pickle plate. "We going back to the beach?"

"Yes," said Aunt Lily Pearl. "Wash your hands. Where's Lily Pearl? She needs to clean up, too."

Howard stood on tiptoe at the sink, holding his hands under the running faucet. "I don't know."

Iva's mother stopped, her hand on the refrigerator door. "What do you mean?"

"I don't know where she went."

"Is she in the house?" Iva's mother asked. "In our room, maybe?"

Howard shook his head. "No. Outside."

Mrs. Honeycutt rushed out the back door, calling Lily Pearl's name. Minutes later, she came back in through the front door and said, "I don't see her anywhere."

Everyone froze. Iva could hear the clock ticking.

Aunt Sissy Two pulled Howard away from the sink and kneeled down. "Are you and Lily Pearl playing a game? Tell me."

He hooked his finger in his bottom lip, afraid he'd done something wrong. "I didn't do nothing.

Honest. Lily Pearl told me she was gonna do like the ice cream."

Iva's mother shot a glance at Aunt Sissy Two. "The ice cream? What's he talking about?"

Iva remembered the first night on the board-walk when they all had gotten frozen custard. Her mother had told Lily Pearl to eat hers before the frozen custard melted. Iva could see Lily Pearl making little legs with her fingers at the pointed tip of her cone.

"She ran away," Iva said, her words falling like bricks. "Lily Pearl ran away."

Chapter Eleven

The National Bank of Heaven

Everyone hurried out the front door to search for Lily Pearl.

"Look everywhere," Iva's mother said. "She might be hiding."

Hunter and Heaven covered both side yards. Iva and Arden checked the backyard. Iva parted the thick snowball bushes, but no Lily Pearl crouched behind them.

"Not in the backyard," Arden reported to their mother.

"Or front yard," Iva's mother said, her voice rising in distress. "I even looked in the cars. Where can she be?"

"Mama, it's Lily Pearl," said Arden. "She runs off every five minutes back home. Remember the time she ran away because we had pork chops?"

"Yes, but that's back home. Everybody in town knows her."

Aunt Sissy Two put her hand on Iva's mother's shoulder. "She can't have gone far. It hasn't been that long since she left."

"We could walk around the neighborhood," Iva suggested.

"The area is too big," Iva's mother said. "She could be on the boardwalk or on the beach or—" She didn't say, *in the water*, but Iva guessed.

Aunt Sissy Two took charge. "Sissy, go inside and call the beach patrol and wait for them here. They'll need a description of Lily Pearl. Plus, she may come back."

"What about us?" Hunter asked. "Should we each take a different street?"

"I'll cruise the neighborhood in my car and take Howard with me," said Aunt Sissy Two. "Hunter, you and Arden hit the boardwalk."

"Go in the gift shops," Iva's mother instructed. "Any place that might sell jewelry. She's been pitching a fit over some kind of necklace."

Iva was stung by a pang of guilt. Lily Pearl had believed that Iva was going to buy her the pearl bride necklace. And she had let Lily Pearl think it. Now it was almost time to go back home. Lily Pearl knew Iva wasn't going to buy her the bride necklace. So it was Iva's fault Lily Pearl had run away.

Iva's mother hustled back indoors. Aunt Sissy Two and Howard got in the car and drove off. Arden and Hunter raced up Bayview Avenue toward the boardwalk.

"What about the beach? Shouldn't we look there?" Iva asked her mother. She and Heaven had followed her into the house. But her mother was busy dialing the phone.

They needed more people, Iva decided. She dashed into the kitchen and grabbed the key ring from the drawer. Back in the living room, she unlocked the door to the upstairs.

"You can't go up there," Heaven said. "It's against the rules."

"This is an emergency." Iva took the steps two at a time.

Mr. Smith crouched on a brown rug in the sitting room. For the first time, Iva got a good look at him. He had floppy blond hair and unblinking blue eyes. He wore a polo shirt and brown-and-gray plaid shorts and was perfectly still.

He was so still that Iva wondered if he was alive. She poked his shoulder with one finger.

"Darn," he said, blinking at last. "You could see me?"

"Uh . . . yeah." This was the brilliant explorer-spy? "My little sister is missing. Will you help us look for her?"

"The little girl with the blond ponytail?" Mr. Smith got up. "I've seen her and the little boy playing in the yard."

"Mama's calling the beach patrol," Iva said. "But it's a big place—"

Mr. Smith raced out of the room and clattered downstairs ahead of her. When he saw Iva's mother in their living room, he said, "Reed Smith. I've just heard about the little girl. I'll drive the girls to the beach. Save some time."

Iva's mother hesitated. Then she said, "Thank you!"

As Iva and Heaven slid into the front seat of Mr. Smith's car, a tan SUV marked BEACH PATROL pulled into the driveway of their house.

"Those are great rescue people," Mr. Smith said, backing his car out onto the street, "but we may find your sister first."

Mr. Smith parked in the first open space and jumped out. "I'll search this end of the beach." He pointed to the short stretch of sand below the boardwalk and jogged off.

"Let's split up," Iva told Heaven.

"If we stay together we'll have a better chance of seeing her. You know, power in numbers."

"I thought that was 'safety in numbers,'" said Iva, but she was glad of Heaven's solid presence. Her cousin might have been bossy, but she was also levelheaded.

The beach was jammed with people lying under umbrellas or on blankets, playing Frisbee, building sand castles, picking up shells, eating, talking, and laughing.

Iva wondered how they'd ever find a five-year-old in this mob.

When she reached the lifeguard stand, she asked Mike if he could help.

"I can't leave my post," he said, watching the swimmers in the water. "But the beach patrol is first-rate. They find lost kids all the time. If I see your sister, I'll wave my flag."

"Thanks." Iva plodded through the sand, scanning the crowd for Lily Pearl's ponytail and blue bathing suit.

Heaven pointed. "Hey, there's London! Maybe she's seen Lily Pearl!"

London Howdyshell jogged toward them. She wore a red-and-white-striped shirt like Heaven's and a frown.

"Where have you been?" she asked Heaven.

"It's almost one thirty. The boat is about to leave."

"I forgot!" Heaven said. "We've been looking for Lily Pearl. She ran away."

"That's too bad," said London, without a trace of sympathy. "I'm sure she'll turn up. C'mon, we have to hurry. Mom and Dad are waiting at the dock."

Iva wondered why she had ever wanted London for her best friend. And couldn't Heaven see that London was even bossier than Heaven was?

Heaven stared openmouthed at London. "It's Lily Pearl. My cousin. She's five. I have to help look for her."

London shrugged. "Suit yourself." She skipped off in the direction of the dock.

"You just gave up your free boat ride," said Iva.

"Did you really think I'd go off with Lily Pearl missing?" Heaven gave Iva a little shove. "Let's haul freight. We're burning daylight."

Iva led the way toward the water. For the first time, she understood the expression her mother often used, *Blood is thicker than water*. Families were more important than friends.

"Maybe she's not even on the beach," Heaven said after they'd reached the water's edge. "It's pretty far for Lily Pearl to walk down here by herself."

"Have you ever seen Lily Pearl when she's in one of her snits? That kid can travel when she's mad about something."

"If only we had some idea where she went."

The boat tooted its horn. Iva watched the *Chesapeake Zephyr* push away from the dock and steam out into the bay. She saw London's red-and-white-striped shirt on the top deck. Was that another girl with her? Iva couldn't tell for sure.

"If only London was with us," Heaven said. "She'd figure out where Lily Pearl went in two seconds."

"I wouldn't count on London." Iva hopped over a pile of wet sand being excavated by a boy of about Howard's age.

Then she stopped to think. The mound of

sand reminded her of the day she'd helped Howard dig his hole. Lily Pearl had picked through the rocks on the sand mountain by Howard's pit and thought she'd found a pearl. Iva had told her that pearls were made by live oysters that lived in the water.

Lily Pearl had also admired London's shark's-tooth necklace that London claimed she had made herself. If Lily Pearl couldn't afford the pearl necklace—and if she figured Iva wouldn't get it for her—she'd try to find a pearl and make a necklace herself.

"She's here on the beach!" Iva blurted. "Near the water."

Heaven grabbed Iva's arm. "D'you see her?"

"No, but I bet she's somewhere along the water. She's looking for oysters."

"Oysters?"

Iva twisted around, trying to peer between all the people at the water's edge. She wished she could climb Mike's lifeguard stand. Up there, she'd be able to see most of the beach. Then she spied the fishing pier. It was pretty high.

"C'mon!" She led the way down the beach and up the steps of the fishing pier.

Heaven headed for the end, where fishermen had leaned their poles against the rail.

"I'll ask those men if they've seen Lily Pearl."

Iva clambered up onto the wide railing near the steps. She had a good view of the half-moon-shaped beach. She roofed her eyes with her hand against the bright sun, but there were still too many people milling around.

Discouraged, she gazed out over the bay. The choppy water was dappled by shifting shadows that reminded her of ancient sailing ships.

Maybe it hadn't been so easy for Captain John Smith, either. He didn't have flashlights and cameras and radios, like modern explorers. In those days, discoverers had to be extra smart.

In the back of her brain, Iva had stored explorers' tricks she'd learned from her old *National Geographic* magazines. She pulled out the one for seeing long-distance when you didn't have binoculars.

She made a tight circle of her index finger and held it up to her right eye. Squinting through it, she scanned each person on the beach. Red-haired woman, kid with a face like a pie pan, man with a big potbelly . . .

And there, bent over by the stone jetty, was a little girl in a bright blue satin two-piece bathing suit. The end of the girl's long blond ponytail was wet.

"I see her!" she cried. She had made her greatest discovery: her lost sister.

Heaven thudded down the wooden planks. "Where? Where is she?"

"Follow me!" Iva leaped off the railing and headed for the jetty at a dead run.

Lily Pearl stood knee-deep in the water, scooping sand and shells into Howard's bucket. When she spotted Iva, she dropped the bucket and burst into tears.

"Don't tell on me," she begged.

Iva hugged Lily Pearl first; then Heaven

hugged her, and then Iva hugged her again.

"Lily Pearl," Iva said. "We've been looking all over for you! Don't you know how worried we've all been?"

Lily Pearl sobbed, "I was trying to find one of those shells with a pearl inside! So I could make a bride necklace."

Heaven elbowed Iva. "You were right! She was looking for oysters."

Iva knelt down and took her sister by the shoulders. "Lily Pearl, you shouldn't have run off."

"But I want a bride necklace!" Lily Pearl stuck the fingers of one hand in her mouth.

Iva pulled her sister's hand out of her

mouth. "Listen, I'll buy you the pearl necklace we saw in the shop."

"You said that before!"

"This time, cross my heart and hope to die." Iva sketched an imaginary cross over her chest.

"Really?" Lily Pearl slipped her spitty hand in Iva's. "I didn't mean it when I said you weren't my favorite sister."

Iva figured Lily Pearl would change her mind again when she found out Iva hadn't robbed a bank or discovered buried treasure in the last thirty minutes. Where would she get the money? She owed everyone but Howard's hermit crab. But she had to buy Lily Pearl that necklace. Period.

"I've got enough to buy it," Heaven said, as if reading Iva's mind.

"Did I hear right? You're actually going to let me have nineteen dollars?" Iva said in disbelief.

"I have to charge interest. But I'll give you a family discount," Heaven added generously.

"How much interest?"

"Fifteen percent."

"Fifteen percent of nineteen dollars is . . ." Iva tried to work out the math in her head, but the small corner of her brain that was assigned to numbers came up empty.

"Two dollars and eighty-five cents," said Heaven. She obviously stored numbers in the front of her brain. "After you get the necklace, I'll still have enough to treat London to the arcade tonight."

So Heaven hadn't noticed the other girl with London. Maybe Iva had imagined it. She wished someone would treat her to the arcade, but she was grateful her cousin was bailing her out.

"You're always loaded with cash," Iva said. "Are you a bank or something?"

"Yes." Heaven grinned. "The National Bank of Heaven."

Chapter Twelve

Captain Iva Honeysuckle Smith

"Can I have another cocktail, please?" Iva drained her glass, and the ice clacked against her teeth. Then she popped the sweet red cherry she had saved for last into her mouth.

From across the table, Heaven watched Iva as she sipped her Coke. Iva was the only one drinking a Shirley Temple.

"Don't fill up on drinks," Iva's mother told Iva. "You ordered a big dinner."

The Honeycutts had taken over the largest outdoor table at the Crab Shack, right next to the boardwalk. Iva's mother had invited Mr. Reed Smith to join them.

But Iva was the star. She felt as famous as Captain John Smith.

The best part of dinner at the Crab Shack

wasn't being the hero for finding Lily Pearl. No, the best part was sitting next to Mr. Smith. It was even worth taking a shower and washing her hair.

The waiter handed Iva a second pink bubbly drink. She gave the little paper umbrella to Lily Pearl.

Lily Pearl twirled it over Howard's head. The pearl on her silver chain gleamed in the lamplight. "I now pronounce us wife and husband!"

Iva felt fizzy with questions. "What were you doing when we came into your room today?" she asked Mr. Smith.

"I was trying to blend in with the rug," he said. "Kind of an experiment."

"You didn't seem very surprised to see us," said Heaven.

"Iva's been in my room before, haven't you?" he asked her. "I noticed my camera had been moved. You seem to be the nosiest, so I figured it was you."

Iva didn't know whether to feel flattered or insulted. She made a note to cover her tracks better when she snuck around in the future.

"You're an explorer-spy," she said. "I found a paper in your garbage can with stuff about not being seen and following your route at night. It's okay, you can tell me. We have almost the same job."

Mr. Smith laughed. "I volunteer for the Virginia Department of Game and Inland Fisheries. I'm working on the Toad and Frog Calling Survey."

"You call frogs?" Arden asked.

"No," he said. "I listen to them. Every year I spend a few weeks listening for different species of frogs and toads. This time I was assigned a route in the marshes around Stingray Point. I go out at night and record the types of frogs and toads I hear call. The survey helps us keep track of different species, in case they change habitats."

"We hear peepers in the spring," said Aunt Sissy Two, "but we don't know about other frogs."

"There are twenty-seven species of frogs and toads in Virginia," Mr. Smith stated. "My specialty is the Fowler's toad. When you approach them, they become motionless and blend in with their backgrounds."

"Your experiment!" Iva cried. "You were being a Fowler's toad!"

"You should hear a Fowler's toad. Sounds like a human scream—very eerie at night. People have been known to call the police, thinking a person's in trouble."

No little toad could have made the racket Iva had heard on Mr. Smith's CD player.

Nudging him, she said quietly, "I've seen her, too."

"Seen who?"

"You know." Iva tried to wink, but she hadn't yet mastered that talent. Instead, she blinked both eyes, like a bullfrog.

Just then, the waiter brought their dinners. Iva had ordered fried scallops after Mr. Smith assured her that scallops were like stingrays, only tastier. After one bite, Iva decided that when she grew up she would dine only on fried scallops and Critch Jackson's barbecued chicken and drink only Shirley Temples.

Iva saw London approaching them. She kicked Heaven's shin under the table. "Your friend's here."

Heaven's face lit up like Christmas morning, and she jumped up from her chair.

London wasn't alone. Another girl was with her. The one from the boat.

"Hey!" Heaven said, pathetically eager. "Want to go to the arcade? My treat."

"No, thanks." London looked at Heaven like she was a cafeteria monitor. "Delia and I are going to hang out. We met on the boat."

Heaven's eagerness slid from her face like a mud pie off a plate as she watched London and Delia leave, laughing like best friends.

"She didn't even say good-bye," Heaven said in a small voice. Iva felt bad for her.

When the chocolate pecan pie arrived, piled high with whipped cream, Iva's mother declared that they needed a family picture.

"But I haven't been able to find my camera in days," she said. "I can't imagine where it went."

Iva couldn't stand it any longer. The guilt of losing her mother's camera was a monstrous weight. It would loom over Iva every waking minute. She had to confess. No punishment would be any worse than living in constant fear.

But she'd have to tell her mother the whole truth. It would get ugly, but she'd have to do it. She ate a bite of her chocolate pecan pie, the last dessert she'd probably have for the next fifty years.

"Mama—" she began.

"Aunt Sissy," Heaven broke in, "I took your camera."

Iva's fork clattered on her plate.

"What?" said Iva's mother and Iva at the same time.

"I'm sorry, Aunt Sissy," Heaven barreled on. "I should have asked to borrow it. But I saw a baby seagull and I wanted a picture of it. I took your camera from your bag."

"Heaven!" said Aunt Sissy Two. "You know better!"

Iva's mother asked, "Where is my camera now?"

"It's gone," Heaven replied. She didn't blink, Iva noticed, a sure sign of telling a lie. "When I went up to the baby seagull, its mother saw me and got mad. She took the camera right out of my hands and flew off! I'm so sorry! It's all my fault."

"Seagulls do protect their young," said Mr. Smith. "But that's quite a story."

"Yes, isn't it?" Iva's mother leaned back, her expression skeptical.

Iva admired Heaven's creative lie, but she

couldn't understand why her cousin was taking the fall for her.

"Heaven, you'll have to pay for Aunt Sissy's camera," said Aunt Sissy Two.

Heaven picked at the tablecloth. "I don't have any money. Aunt Sissy, are you going to send me to jail?"

"No," said Aunt Sissy. "I'm sending you to the garden. You'll work off the cost of the camera by pulling weeds and picking vegetables."

"Want some company?" Iva heard herself blurt. She hated working in the hot, buggy garden and would almost rather have gone to jail. But she couldn't let Heaven take the whole punishment.

Heaven flashed her Sunday-school smile. "Yeah. Thanks."

Iva finished her pie, wondering why Heaven had stuck her neck out for her. Was it possible she and Heaven were getting along again? Or did Heaven just want something?

"Let's walk on the beach one last time," Arden suggested.

"Good idea," said Aunt Sissy Two. "We can use the exercise after that dinner."

Mr. Smith had to leave for his frog-and-toad route. He shook Iva's hand and wished her luck. Iva had already figured she'd have to make her own luck.

On the beach, they all took off their shoes. The damp sand felt cool on Iva's bare feet as she walked along the water's edge. A full moon ducked behind a hazy cloud.

The others lagged behind with Aunt Sissy Two and Iva's mother, but Iva skipped ahead to the dock. She ran out to the end and leaned over the rail.

The water was as dark as the night. The only lights were from some far-off boats.

Waves shhh-shhushed against the piers. Iva heard something else, too. A soft splash, like a giant paddle hitting the water.

She strained to see in the inky blackness. Something rose from the water, big enough to block out the lights from the distant boats. Iva sensed the presence of a long, smooth neck and a small head, turned toward her. Then it slid back into the water without a ripple.

Iva whispered, "Bye!"

Iva sat squished in the backseat of her mother's car. Wedged between her and Heaven was a large box containing Heaven's daisy-embroidered sheets, Iva's *National Geographic* magazines, her discovery shorts and discovery journal that she never used, the seashell-covered trinket box Heaven had bought for Miz Compton, Howard's jar of sand from the sand hole he'd dug, and Lily Pearl's enormous collection of dull seashells.

"I need more room." Heaven began complaining before they were out of the driveway of the beach house. "Iva, move over."

"I can barely breathe now," Iva said. "You're bigger than when we came. You know what they say: vacations are broadening."

"I haven't gained an ounce," Heaven said huffily.

Arden, who sat in the front seat, asked her mother, "How come I can't ride in Aunt Sissy Two's car with Hunter?"

"Don't worry. I doubt we'll get five miles before we have to stop and change kids." Mrs. Honeycutt turned the car left onto Bayview Avenue, heading home.

At the risk of damaging a kidney, Iva twisted around to wave out the back windshield. "Bye, Chesapeake Bay! Bye, Heron's Rest!"

"Herons were the only things that could rest in that house," Iva's mother said. "Vacations are exhausting."

"Mama, do you think my legs are my best feature?" Arden asked.

"Arden, I'm driving."

Arden turned to Iva. "Are my legs good? Tell me the truth."

Iva didn't know how to answer this. "Well . . . they do a good job of holding you up. But your knees are square."

"My knees are not square! Oh! They are, kind

of. Mama, I have square knees! I'll never get a boyfriend."

Iva leaned back. They had only been at Stingray Point for five days. But everybody had been different while they were there.

Arden and Hunter had become boy-crazy. Lily Pearl had gone pearl-crazy. Howard wouldn't leave his hole. Boring old Heaven had become adventurous! Would everyone go back to their regular selves once they got home?

Iva decided she was a little bit broader, too. Not in shape, but she had learned to stand on top of something high and get a wider view of the world, and then see people one at a time, as if through an index-finger peephole.

She still didn't know why Heaven had taken the blame for the camera. Maybe she'd felt sorry for Iva. Or maybe they had more in common than just being family. When they got home, Iva would find out the truth.

Heaven rooted through the box between them, pulling out a tablet and pencil. She propped the tablet on her lap and flipped to the first page.

"You're not making more Daily Life cards, are you?" Iva asked.

"No, I'm making you a payment booklet."

"A what?"

"For your loan. Like Daddy has for his truck," Heaven explained. "He mails a ticket when he makes his truck payment."

She printed *The National Bank of Heaven* across the top. "I'm making ten tickets. You should be able to pay me back nineteen dollars plus interest in ten payments."

Clearly, Heaven was already back to her regular self.

Iva ran her tongue over her front teeth. Her mother had made her take a shower and wash her hair. But Iva still hadn't brushed her teeth. Not for five glorious days.

"Hey."

Heaven looked up from making Iva's payment booklet.

Iva flashed a big smile, revealing her grossly coated teeth.

"*Ew!*" Heaven squealed. "Aunt Sissy! Iva hasn't brushed her teeth in forever! They're green!"

"Iva . . ." her mother said in a tone that indicated it would be a very long drive home.

Iva settled back again. Captain John Smith probably hadn't brushed his teeth when he was

exploring that river with two *p*'s and two *n*'s. If it was good enough for him, it was good enough for her, Captain Iva Honeysuckle Smith.

"And don't you go blowing your rotten breath all over me, either," Heaven snorted.

Iva grinned to herself. Some things never changed.